MICHAEL SUMLER

The Cheese Hustle

Everyday is a new pizza. You can
change the toppings, the crust, the
style. But the secret ingredient remains you.

— Lenny Bruno

Just Another Day in Pizza Paradise

Today is just another ordinary day for forty-year-old Lenny Burno, as his car wheezes through Baltimore like an asthmatic dinosaur. He swears it's faster than a bus, if only buses didn't have schedules. The engine coughs each time he misses a turn, and Lenny's convinced the clanging is some new GPS feature, telling him how many blocks he's gone too far.

His phone vibrates furiously from the chaos on his dashboard. He glances at it: J. Watkins, his landlord, no extra charge. But Lenny's not biting. Motivational wisdom spills through his car speakers, scrambled and crackling. "Turn setbacks into comebacks," advises the podcast. "Turn setbacks into pizza-backs," translates Lenny, almost proudly.

His dashboard resembles a chaotic war zone, littered with crumpled pizza-delivery receipts and empty energy drink cans that rattle like a swarm of rats in a tin can. A bobblehead slice of pizza teeters precariously with every jolt from the potholes, as if cheerleading his reckless journey. The steering wheel clings to his fingers, coated in a sticky residue he whimsically believes brings him fortune, while a flattened pack of gum stubbornly adheres to the fabric of his seat, fighting for its place in the cluttered chaos.

Lenny's phone keeps buzzing—watertight evidence that he's

the most wanted man in Baltimore, at least by one person who expects rent money.

He's a speed demon at twenty miles an hour, braking just in time to miss another turn. The old self-help podcast can't decide if it wants to play or skip a beat. The voice stutters, "When one door closes," and Lenny thinks it's going to suggest a back window, but it fizzles out, leaving him with his favorite part—the guessing.

His uniform is a showcase of Baltimore's finest pizza chains: faded red polo from Uncle Sal's on top, competing with mustard-yellow pants from Doughboys. An embroidered "L. Br" suggests the most letters he's committed to one job, and mismatched buttons serve as job security, showing off his position as a delivery free agent. He smells like he took a bath in garlic butter and uses the cheesy aroma like personal branding. The pizza-shaped air freshener sways optimistically but doesn't stand a chance.

The Podcast snaps back to life, and he tries to catch it with the sincerity of a man catching a foul ball at the World Series. "Success isn't the absence of problems," it says, "it's the presence of mind."

Lenny grins. Success is a car filled with empty cans, crackling speakers, and an exasperated landlord. But he knows what it really means: where others see obstacles, he sees free parking. He nods along, making mental notes on how to sell the concept back to Tony.

The engine's sputtering reminds him of his ex-girlfriend's mother's asthmatic pug, only less reliable. But as far as Lenny's concerned, it's the tune of the underdog—struggling, scrappy, always on the edge of something great, like winning a pizza lottery. His optimism steers him around corners even faster than his bald tires.

The phone buzzes again. Lenny doesn't need to see the screen to know it's Watkins, more persistent than a meat-lover's special. Lenny wonders if his landlord is aware of the philosophical implications of not picking up—surely that's more meaningful than sending a check. He's doing him a favor, really, making sure the man's life isn't burdened by predictability.

"Turn mistakes into victories," crackles the voice over his speakers, with the enthusiasm of someone who's never been fired six times in ten years.

"Turn stakes into deliveries," Lenny upgrades, watching a couple stroll by on the sidewalk. He shakes his head at their traditional approach to walking, two legs and all. Some people just don't get efficiency.

His car groans, his phone buzzes, and a man yells from a stoop that Lenny missed another turn. But Lenny just grins and guns the engine. Opportunity is like a pizza—hot and fast—and he's determined to deliver.

Lenny skids his car to a halt outside a building so decrepit even roaches have given up and moved to the suburbs. He grabs the pizza box and catapults himself over a puddle that might be conducting science experiments on itself. Just as he reaches the door, a delivery bike with more rust than frame narrowly misses him. A tired-eyed tenant answers, staring at Lenny like he's delivering subpoenas instead of dinner.

"What's with the extra anchovies?" The tenant glances inside the box, then jabs it with a finger as if it owes him money.

Lenny unleashes his best customer service grin, "Anchovy about that!" he says, not missing a beat. "Guess the chef was feeling extra saucy today!" He holds the pizza out like an Olympic torch, but the tenant doesn't seem impressed by the runner or the sport. The guy's wearing a shirt with more holes than fabric and an expression to match.

"You gonna fix it, or just stand there delivering punchlines?" says the tenant. He looks like he hasn't been impressed since the Reagan administration.

"We fix it, it's another thirty minutes. That pizza gets cold, we've got a Code Red on our hands. You'll have to chew through an iceberg," Lenny says. His arms are getting tired, but his smile isn't. "Tell you what," he continues, "next time, toppings are on me. Delivery guaranteed!"

The tenant narrows his eyes, the universal signal for evaluating how much a person's soul is worth. He hands Lenny a crumpled bill that looks like it survived several wars.

"Some tip," he says to himself. *"Not enough for pizza college."*

Lenny takes the money, wincing like it physically hurts, which it does. But before his pride took a nosedive, he plastered on another grin and saluted the guy with the same enthusiasm he might for a four-star general.

The door thuds closed behind him, and Lenny remains frozen in place, his shoulders slumping as if the weight of defeat has settled on them. He glances at the crumpled bills in his hand, their crisp edges contrasting sharply with the chaos of his life. The numbers dance in his mind like errant pepperoni slices; calculating how many deliveries it would take to scrape together rent feels like a riddle he can't solve. Math was never his strong suit—more of a pizza pie guy than a number cruncher.

He shoves the tip in his pocket and takes a deep breath, resetting himself like a 1990s Tamagotchi.

"Every pizza rejection is just a slice of redirection," he mutters. "Obstacles are opportunities in cheese's clothing."

With his internal battery recharged, he bounds back to the car. It coughs and complains, but he knows the tune. It's the underdog theme song, and he's the most dedicated fan.

Lenny leaps into the driver's seat and jabs at the ignition, his fingers fumbling with the stubborn key. It jams halfway in, and for a fleeting moment, he glances skyward as if seeking cosmic guidance. But then, a grin breaks across his face, fueled by an unshakeable optimism. He twists the key with all the conviction of a motivational speaker rallying a crowd, and after a few sputtering coughs, the engine bursts to life with a triumphant growl that reverberates through the rusted chassis.

He takes off again, zipping through the streets of Baltimore, where the air carries the faint stench of every imaginable topping—an unpaid power bill swirling in his wake.

The door chime at Martinelli's Pizzeria erupts into a cacophony of frantic jingles as Lenny crashes through. Flour-dusted employees freeze mid-knead, glancing around as if waiting for the ground to shake or a crew of mobsters to storm in. Instead, it's just Lenny—again. He bursts in like a whirlwind, trailing an air of breathless excitement and wild energy, reminiscent of a high school pep rally spiraling out of control.

"Timer!" Lenny shouts, waving like the kitchen's on fire, which it might be.

His boss, Tony Martinelli, stood like a squinting pizza general, surveying the battlefield. Lenny reached the counter and unleashed his newest scheme.

"Imagine it: pizza parkour! An app called Slice Routes!" He's got enough enthusiasm to fuel the whole block.

The small kitchen buzzes with awkward excitement. A teen in a flour-covered apron whispers to his coworker and jabs a finger toward Lenny like he's sighting Bigfoot. Lenny doesn't notice or care; he's in the zone.

"Listen, Tony, I've got this thing all mapped out!" Lenny said, bouncing on his heels like he's about to break into dance. "Every shortcut in Baltimore is precision-timed to the second. Delivery drivers pay us to get their routes!" His arms sliced the air, sketching out his imaginary empire, narrowly missing Tony's nose.

Tony watched, a sculpture of unimpressed authority, waiting for Lenny to run out of steam or air, whichever comes first.

"Bruno," he finally said, shaking his head. "I can't keep up with your innovations. Or your gas money."

But Lenny wasn't done yet. He waved Tony off and kept talking. "We get investors! We go public! This could be the next Mozzarella of Wall Street!" Lenny's passion was radioactive, and the entire kitchen paused to soak in the glow.

"Next thing I know, you'll be selling shares in anchovies," Tony replied, deadpan.

Lenny blinks like Tony just revealed the secret of life. "We can do that?"

"Why not?" Tony shrugged. "More solid than your last ten ideas. All combined."

The other staff dodged Lenny's orbit like planets circling a particularly chaotic sun. One attempted to save a stack of pizza boxes, but Lenny's flailing arms sent them crashing to the floor like fallen dominoes.

Lenny swooped down to help, grabbing the boxes with the urgency of a paramedic saving lives. "Don't worry, I've got it!" he insisted, re-stacking them in the wrong order, while employees exchanged glances that spoke volumes about what it was like working there.

"You ever gonna listen, Bruno?" Tony asked. "Your deliveries are faster than your attention span."

The words didn't pierce Lenny's force field. "Timing is everything," Lenny insisted, rising to his feet. "You of all people should have known that, Timer!" He shot finger guns, feigning ignorance of his lack of impact.

Tony stayed calm, letting Lenny's chaos bounce off his veteran's resolve. The kitchen was back in motion, but all eyes remained on the sideshow.

"Fine," Lenny said, as if agreeing to let everyone else be wrong. "You'll see. This time next year, I'll be eating pepperoni at the top."

"Order me a slice from the bottom," Tony replied. "That's where you'll be sitting."

Lenny opened his mouth, ready to deliver a show-stopping pitch, but instead, a ball of dough smacked him squarely in the chest. Tony's aim was legendary in the pizzeria world, and Lenny had learned that the hard way. He stared down at the floury handprint blooming on his uniform, his lips moving silently as if he were rehearsing new slogans: Pizza Back Guarantee. Extra Dough for the Bold.

"And be sure to take that next delivery. If the customer complained, it was coming out of your pepperoni," Tony said with a smile, nodding at the next delivery.

"Fine," Lenny said, louder this time. Without another word, he took hold of the order and stormed toward the door, pointing at Tony with exaggerated suspicion. "Small-time thinkers!"

The door slammed behind him with all the drama of a B-movie villain.

In the car, he pressed play on the podcast again, his fingers tapping nervously against the steering wheel. The familiar voice filled the space, promising to unveil the secrets of success. Lenny leaned forward in his seat, eyes wide with anticipation, convinced that any moment now, a golden nugget of wisdom would reveal itself like a hidden treasure waiting just for him.

The Mansion That Wasn't There

The wheel squirmed in his hands like it knew he didn't have a plan. Lenny held on, chasing enlightenment, and turned the volume up until his windows rattled. The voice crackled, filling his car like the smell of anticipation. When life gives you anchovies, make—static—opportunity pizza! This time, he didn't need to guess the conclusion. His grin stretched wider than his rent was overdue, racing past the trees as they sprinted away. The mansion loomed, huge and ominous, like a surprise pizza party that didn't order enough plates. He checked the address and decided to go for it anyway.

He pumped the gas pedal, treating his car like a racehorse instead of a glue factory reject. The trees turned to green blurs on either side, and he hunched over the wheel, his bald head catching the faint afternoon light. Lenny held the phone to his face, triple-checking the delivery address. He read it, then read it again. The screen didn't change, not even to complain about an unpaid bill. The mansion loomed closer, eating the landscape. His brain buzzed as much as his car, processing the situation like an order gone very wrong. But if something was this out of place, Lenny figured, it was probably fate, like the universe begging him to deliver.

The GPS hiccuped, his car ached, but Lenny pushed forward.

He squinted at the huge building, and the doubt in his head started jumping up and down like an over-caffeinated customer service rep. This wasn't a home; it was a city block disguised as a mansion. It cast long shadows across the land, and his confidence cowered underneath. He rubbed the back of his neck with his free hand and winced. Delivery guaranteed, he told himself, remembering Tony's parting words like a mantra. Order me a slice from the bottom. It played on a loop in his mind, louder than the clanging from his engine.

An iron gate sprouted from nowhere, eager to get in his way. It loomed, just as daunting as the mansion, with spiked tips and a stern look about it. Lenny slowed and looked over his shoulder, briefly considering turning back. He shook his head, dismissing the thought like a disappointing appetizer. That wasn't how a real entrepreneur behaved. He knew that better than anyone. After all, opportunity was opportunity, even if it involved driving through something that looked like the entrance to a gothic theme park.

He patted the dashboard and coaxed the car toward the gate. It didn't open, but it didn't need to; it merely sat there with quiet disdain. His underdog of a vehicle squeaked through the narrow opening, Lenny maneuvering like it was a pizza box squeezed into a narrow fridge shelf. The car protested with the automotive equivalent of wheezing, but Lenny didn't let that stop him. The road was like the twisty straw in his grape soda, winding with too many turns and getting narrower as he went. He watched the mansion come back into view, big and foreboding. It glared at him like it didn't care for cheesy toppings, and his instincts sent one last desperate signal: suspicious.

The mansion crept up to meet him, much too friendly for

Lenny's liking. It sat there, too big and too fancy, like the kind of thing you read about in billionaire gossip magazines. Lenny parked, barely making it into a spot near the grand entrance. He sat in the car, trying to figure out if this was the mother of all setups. A moment of doubt sneaked in, but he pushed it away. His enthusiasm was a heavyweight champion, even if the rest of him felt like an amateur. He grabbed the pizzas, and the steam reminded him that it was now or never. With one last glance at the address, he leaped out of the car, the warm light from the mansion washing over him like a neon OPEN sign.

Lenny stood in the driveway, staring up at the mansion like he was David sizing up Goliath, if Goliath had marble columns and custom landscaping. His underdog nature rebelled against the opulence, but the ambition in him saw a giant that needed toppling. He took a deep breath and talked himself into courage. You got this, he thought, like he was reading from a self-help book for pizza delivery drivers. His car, parked crookedly, looked like a forgotten toy in the land of rich giants. Lenny imagined he'd become part of an elaborate prank and briefly thought about ditching the whole thing and spending his evening dodging Tony's badgering instead.

The steam rising from the boxes made him bold. If this was the big time, he wasn't about to let a little thing like his complete lack of preparedness stop him. The pizzas felt like they weighed a hundred pounds, but the weight was nothing compared to his optimism. This was a new frontier, and Lenny was determined to stake his claim, even if the stake came with extra cheese and pepperoni.

His air freshener swung wildly, matching the pounding of his heart as he strode across the gravel. The pizzas burned his hands, but they were the kind of burns that paid off, like scalding yourself with fresh pie. Each step brought him closer, his disheveled uniform clinging to him like a security blanket. He watched his feet make prints on the driveway, then disappear, dwarfed by the vastness of the mansion. It seemed more immense with every step, and he felt more determined. Lenny climbed the final set of stairs to the porch, huffing a little but triumphant. The door was within reach now, and so was the delivery of a lifetime.

He pushed the doorbell like a car horn. The chime reverberated through the mansion, grand and dignified, making Lenny's presence feel like a spaghetti stain on a tuxedo. Before he could gather himself or a convincing excuse to leave, the door swung open. An older man in a suit worth more than Lenny's lifetime of wages appeared. Lenny hesitated, his confidence waning.

"Pardon the intrusion," he said, each word battling its way out, his smile as awkward as a toddler's first steps.

The man nodded, an unspoken question in his eyes, "They are expecting you," he said as he gestured for him to enter.

Lenny stepped inside, trying to act like this was all part of his master plan. His shoes squeaked against the marble floor, each step announcing his presence louder than a megaphone. He was a pizza delivery guy in an opera house, a cheesy thumb in a glittering world. His uniform felt tighter with every step, constricting like a boa on a very nervous mouse. He marveled at the grandeur—crystal chandeliers bigger than his car, statues that probably cost more than his student loans, which wasn't saying much. He fought the urge to ask if they took in strays.

The man gave a slight nod, a gesture that said everything and nothing at the same time. Lenny was pretty sure it meant "Please don't touch anything, and who let you in?"

He nodded back, mimicking a confidence he didn't feel,

and held the pizzas like they were a pair of newborn twins. He followed the quiet hum of conversation, each step a new adventure in anxiety.

He made his way down a long hallway, his heart thumping like a faulty engine. The walls were lined with art—probably originals, he guessed, though what he knew about art could fill a very small, greasy box. He clung to the hope of a tip as generous as the décor, envisioning enough money to float him through rent and maybe even one of those fancy chandeliers.

He passed a grand piano that seemed to mock him with its elegance. His footsteps echoed as he walked, a continuous reminder that he didn't belong. He rounded a corner, the pizza boxes tilting dangerously, when his foot caught on an expensive-looking Persian rug.

The world moved in slow motion.

Lenny lunged forward, the pizzas leaping out of his arms like they had lives of their own. He stumbled, reaching for the boxes but catching only air and a faceful of marble floor. The pizzas arced beautifully, terrifyingly, toward a door that was slightly ajar.

His life flashed before his eyes: missed deliveries, expired coupons, and a giant cardboard question mark. He scrambled to his feet, driven by the horror of letting a pizza go undelivered and the desperation to prevent more chaos. But the pizzas had a will of their own. They sailed through the air like delicious comets, trailing cheesy tails.

The door swung open with perfect timing, and Lenny barreled through, helpless to stop the impending crash.

The boxes exploded on the poker table with a spectacular crash.

Pepperoni rained over the luxury carpet. Steam billowed

around the crystal ashtray. Cheese landed with a sad plop on a mountain of poker chips. Everything was covered, like the toppings of chaos had spilled all over the mansion.

Lenny froze, still trying to comprehend the scene. His presence shattered the room like a wild pitch at a playoff game. Rich wood-paneled walls seemed to close in on him as the players took in the disaster. The world had gone silent, but inside Lenny's head, the chaos screamed like a thousand angry customers.

Olu "O.G." Goldfinger sat at the center of the table, his traditional agbada pristine even amid the carnage. His gaze was a laser, narrowing on Lenny with the calm intensity of a man who'd seen worse and come out winning.

Kim So-yeon was to his left, her perfectly styled bob as unmoving as her hands, which had paused mid-reach for a poker chip. Her lips parted in disbelief, and her eyes widened, trying to process the unexpected turn of events like a complex math problem.

Mr. Saito occupied a corner of the room, the shadowy enigma behind it all. He barely moved, yet his presence loomed, as if he'd orchestrated the entire spectacle.

For one paralyzing moment, everything stopped.

The players were a portrait of shock, frozen like a scene out of a dramatic painting Lenny couldn't afford. Cards and chips, once the sole focus of their attention, lay in a glorious mess of mozzarella and crust. Lenny's heart sank to his feet. He was the new center of their universe, and he didn't like the attention one bit.

He stared back at them, his mind racing through a catalog of excuses, but nothing surfaced that matched the gravity of the situation. His eyes flicked to the side, noticing a small fortune in poker chips representing more money than he'd make in a decade. They lay scattered in the aftermath of his cataclysmic entrance, some tipped with red sauce, others drowning in cheese.

They waited for him to say something, anything. Lenny gulped, feeling the weight of the moment crushing down like a dozen poorly stacked boxes. His cheeks flushed a color he'd only seen on the hottest of pepperonis. He swallowed hard, his mouth suddenly as dry as a leftover crust.

The silence was so complete, it needed its own business card.

Then, without warning, he did what he always did: opened his mouth and hoped for the best.

"That's some icebreaker!" Lenny finally said, the echo louder than a hundred old podcasts.

It felt like an anchovy on a vegan pizza. He moved to collect toppings, only making things worse with each attempt. The players exchanged glances. O.G. laughed, deep and booming.

"You've truly delivered, my friend." Kim's expression flick-ered from shock to amused skepticism.

Mr. Saito leaned forward, commanding attention, a small, knowing smile forming.

Lenny grinned, panic and bravado at war. "Guess I really delivered a hot hand, huh?"

No one laughed this time, and Lenny's smile wavered. The toppings slid through his fingers, each pepperoni landing with a dramatic finality. O.G. watched with an amused twinkle in his eye, a faint chuckle escaping like he found the chaos refreshing. Kim's skepticism was almost palpable, but her lips twitched as if fighting the urge to smile. Lenny scrambled on his hands and knees, desperation creeping in. The room loomed larger with every failed grab at pizza. The more he tried to fix the mess, the worse it got, and the players seemed to be betting on how long it would take him to give up.

He stumbled through a string of jokes, his voice cracking like dry twigs underfoot. The bravado that once rolled off his tongue now felt as fragile as a soggy pizza box, collapsing at the slightest pressure.

"So… I guess this is what you call a surprise topping?" he continued, hoping for a sliver of mercy.

No one replied, but O.G.'s smile didn't fade, and Kim's eyes tracked him with cautious interest. Lenny wiped his forehead, leaving a streak of sauce, and flopped down on the floor in defeat, more pizza on him than in the boxes. It was a delivery to end all deliveries, and Lenny was its most embarrassed recipient.

It was then he really noticed the chips. They lay next to him like miniature towers, mocking his earnings as a pizza man. Each stack screamed wealth, taunting him with what he couldn't reach. The stakes of the game—and the stakes of his interruption—began to dawn on him. He gulped, piecing together the scale of the disaster and feeling like an undercooked crust. This wasn't just any poker game; it was Mount Olympus for gamblers, and he'd crashed it wearing the cheapest toga in Baltimore.

Mr. Saito stepped out of the shadows, his diamond-studded grillz flashing with unsettling authority. The room shifted, all eyes turning to him, including Lenny's. Saito's gaze fell on Lenny, unreadable yet terrifyingly direct. Lenny's heartbeat was a bass drum in a symphony of shame. Silence blanketed the room again, and even the mozzarella stopped sliding. It was Lenny versus the rich and famous, and the odds were as stacked as the chips. He wanted to say more, to do something clever, but his voice was hiding under the table with the rest of him.

Lenny's lips moved soundlessly, his apologies dying in the shadow of Mr. Saito's inscrutable stare. Saito raised a hand, elegant and final, and Lenny fell quiet, uncertain whether he was about to be fed to the dogs or merely kicked to the curb. The atmosphere was as tense as a forgotten rubber band on a takeout menu, waiting to snap.

Then, as if the universe needed to prove its own unpredictability, a single card flipped through the air, twirling with taunting grace before landing on the table. It was an Ace, its presence shocking in its silence. Lenny watched it settle, understanding dawning with the weight of a thousand late rent checks. He wasn't just a minor interruption; he was now a variable, a wild card in their high-stakes game.

O.G. laughed again, the sound full of new meaning. "Looks like the hand has changed, my friend."

Kim tilted her head, curiosity gleaming in her eyes, the skepticism replaced by intrigue. Lenny was paralyzed, not by fear but by a dawning sense of opportunity-or—or maybe just confusion. The other players, previously unnoticed in the corners, exchanged rapid whispers, some seeing him as an amusing anomaly, others as a threat.

Lenny didn't know if he was in on the joke or the butt of it, but his nature was to plunge ahead anyway. Was this a test, a prank, or just his luck, twisting like the streets he knew so well? He had no idea if this was what destiny looked like or if he was about to get kicked out on his pizza-stained pants.

Mr. Saito gestured again, this time towards an empty chair. Lenny's eyes widened. The room was a tension sandwich, with extra suspense and a side of nervous coleslaw. A delivery gone wrong? Maybe. But it wasn't over yet, and Lenny wasn't about to throw in the towel—not when it might be the luckiest hand he'd ever been dealt.

He was ushered to a seat, the expectation almost physical, the room's collective attention wrapping around him like a dozen too-tight uniforms. The game resumed, the cards shuffled and re-dealt, and Lenny was in it, knee-deep in the mozzarella of chance.

He panicked for a second, the gravity of the situation yanking him back. But then he grinned, embracing the chaos as only Lenny could. He had no idea what he was doing, and that's exactly how he liked it. It was a delivery of a lifetime, and for once, he might just come out on top.

A Slice of Opportunity

Mr. Saito spoke first. "This game could be... interesting," he said, the pause longer than the odds of Lenny winning.

"It's a novelty," said Kim So-yeon, grinning as Lenny picked a clump of cheese from his shoe.

"Do you have more surprises for us, my friend?" asked Olu, resting his chin on a massive fist.

Lenny laughed like they were joking, but knew they probably weren't. He flailed for a witty comeback, trying to act cool but succeeding only in adding more stains to his clothes. "Not yet," he said, not sure if he meant it.

He reached for the cards, trying to shuffle them like he'd seen in movies, but his hands were more enthusiastic than skilled. The cards flipped out of control, landing like embarrassing confetti. Lenny's grin stayed on, but it was working overtime, much like him. His thoughts jumped around like untrained fleas. Did they know he wasn't a gambler? Was this a setup, or were they genuinely curious about how long he could last? Kim's smile made him think both.

He panicked, thinking about how often he failed. "You know what my podcast says about odds?" he blurted.

The millionaires watched him with interest, like they were waiting for something else to explode.

"It's the ultimate adventure," he continued. "Beats turning pizzas." His brain was a traffic jam, words crashing into each other. Was this what it felt like to succeed?

His hands shook. Cards slipped out of his grip like hopes, one landing in a crystal ashtray. "I've got nothing!" he declared, arms flung wide like the chaotic map of his life. Kim's laugh was a crisp echo, as refined as the room.

"That's refreshing," said Mr. Saito.

He stared at them, confused and out of things to say. He reached deep into his mind for self-help wisdom, but all he found was the sound of floundering. It was a scene from his worst nightmare, only with better furniture. Yet they watched him with an intensity that was both thrilling and terrifying. How could they be interested in him when he was barely himself?

They waited like Lenny was a complicated math equation that just needed solving. Silence grew like mold on his best shirt. He finally broke, gasping for words like air, "So, uh, as my motivational podcast says, when life gives you tomatoes, you make pizza sauce, right?"

Kim smiled as if he were an especially amusing experiment.

Mr. Saito raised an eyebrow, intrigued by the anomaly in his game.

Olu gave a warm chuckle that didn't quite reassure him.

Maybe he was the delivery.

The door swung open, and a man in a pristine suit stood there, surveying the room as he seemed to glide toward an empty seat around the card table. His eyes settled on the pizza stains with mathematical disgust.

Lenny blinked. "Do you do our taxes?" he asked.

"No," the man said, arranging chips with terrifying precision.

"I do your odds."

The man was stone-faced.

"Slick Vic. Glad you finally arrived," Mr. Saito said. The room said nothing.

"I'm not sure if I should've been even later," Slick Vic murmured, casting another wary glance at Lenny.

The door swung open with a force that rattled the room, causing Lenny to flinch. A captivating woman strode in, her presence commanding attention with every deliberate step. Her luxurious silk robes flowed around her like a cascade of shimmering waves, each fold and drape hinting at a price tag that could cover his rent for years.

"Oh my, hold the anchovies," Lenny thought as he took all of the lady in.

"Who's the owl?" she said, "And didn't your Mama teach you not to stare," seeing Lenny's eyes locked on her.

Lenny's lips snapped shut, his mind racing for words that just wouldn't come.

"Forgive us, Ms. Khadijah al-Hari, this is...sorry, never got your name," Olu said, as he turned to Lenny.

"Uh, yeah, the name's Lenny."

"Yes, this is Lenny, Lenny the delivery guy," Olu continued with a smile.

"Is he part of the game?" she asked.

Lenny wished for an escape hatch. "Guess I am," he mumbled.

"Or just the entertainment?" the woman added, her laugh as sharp as her gaze.

They settled around him, forming a pentagon of power. Lenny felt himself shrink, his presence a small speck on their radar. He grinned nervously and tried to act like he belonged, but they weren't fooled. "Glad you could join," he said. The joke was on him, and he didn't even get the punchline.

Slick Vic edged closer, arranging the table with the efficiency of a machine. Lenny slouched in his chair, feeling like a typo on a crisp document. The man had a mechanical way about him, intense and methodical.

"Welcome to the big game," Vic said.

Lenny tried to match his unblinking stare but failed miserably.

Khadijah was even more intimidating. She moved with authority, each gesture making him smaller. Her outfit glittered, and Lenny thought she might be made of pure currency.

"This should be interesting," she said, her eyes laser-focused on Lenny, dissecting him with precision.

They circled him like rich vultures eyeing a confused rabbit. He melted under the heat, his confidence running like cheap cheese on a hot day. They spoke about him like he wasn't there, bantering back and forth with practiced ease.

"So, we have a surprise addition," said Slick Vic. "Unlikely variable."

"More like an unstable one," replied Khadijah, her laugh the echo of expensive things breaking. Lenny was sweating anchovy oil. He was more of an afterthought than a competitor, and they seemed to relish his discomfort.

"How's a delivery guy compete with you?" he finally piped up, desperate for acknowledgment. His voice quivered like an old cassette tape.

Vic and Khadijah exchanged a knowing look, the kind that cut deeper than any words.

"It could happen," said Vic, doubt dripping from his tongue.

"Once," said Khadijah. "In a dream."

They didn't answer him directly, but they didn't need to. Lenny felt the weight of their eyes, each stare heavier than the last. He looked down at his hands, covered in sauce and failure. The door was so close, but escape felt like a distant fantasy.

A thin sheen of sweat trickled down Lenny's back, saturating his delivery uniform and making the vinyl chair cling uncomfortably to his skin. The five millionaires leaned back in their plush seats, their laughter ringing out like chimes as they exchanged banter and tossed around bets that could buy a small yacht. Lenny felt like a fish floundering on dry land, acutely aware that he was drowning in a sea of wealth and confidence far beyond his reach.

His fingers fumbled with the slick cards, dampened by the clammy grip of anxiety and anticipation. They were indifferent to his pizza-stained existence, their eyes gleaming with calculated odds he couldn't begin to comprehend. The gulf between them was a chasm, and they reveled in it, knowing he was outmatched.

Lenny had never felt like such a vivid underdog, each detail magnified under the harsh fluorescent lights. He glanced at their polished suits and smug smiles, wealth radiating from them like heat from the ancient ovens back at Tony's. They casually stacked chips as if they were mere tokens of amusement, while the room tilted around him, leaving him scrambling to catch up.

"So, Mr. Lenny," Kim began, "what are your life goals?" She leaned forward, eager for data.

"Like... in general?" Lenny stalled. The others stared like a human experiment.

"My calculations say he doesn't have any," Vic interjected.

Lenny scratched his head. "To make money. Or deliver pizza.

Both, I guess." The table raised a collective eyebrow.

"Why not gamble?" Kim persisted. "Statistically speaking, it's fast."

Lenny laughed nervously. "I don't usually win. Unless you count pizza awards, then it's all me." He smiled but somehow still felt exposed.

"I'd count not spilling as a win," said Khadijah. "And you're losing."

Inside, he shrank beneath the weight of their gazes.

The room waited, thick with the weight of the moment. Lenny cracked a smile, his default setting when panicked. "Five-year plan? I'm still working on my five-minute plan not to spill more pizza."

The millionaires didn't blink.

"Guess that's delivery life," he continued, scrambling. "Pizza's more reliable than luck."

"Not for you," Vic calculated, causing laughter to ripple around the table.

Lenny was surrounded. His ambition looked like delivery fliers against their executive reports. He fidgeted under their scrutiny. It felt like they were betting on when he would collapse.

"This is, uh, new for me," he admitted.

"Then try it," Kim encouraged. "You might surprise your-self."

Their attention went back to the cards, giving him room to breathe. He didn't. Instead, he kept talking, his hands moving as fast as his mouth.

"When life gives you dough, make a fortune," he muttered, the self-help wisdom almost comforting.

They regarded him as if he were an exotic animal brought in

for their amusement. Their scrutiny was relentless, each glance a professional interrogation light. Lenny cracked again.

"Delivery isn't gambling," he said, his voice straining under pressure. "I know the odds."

Olu chuckled. "Very observant."

Kim's smile was back. "You might surprise us, too."

Lenny's world spun like a pizza crust, barely holding its shape. They bombarded him with questions, his ambition under a high-powered microscope. They thought he was insane, and maybe he was. He felt smaller with each response.

They laughed, and he tried to take notes on what they thought he should do. Were they making fun of him, or did they really think he could win? He wasn't sure, and that confused him more than the stakes.

His mind ran wild, but didn't go anywhere. "I'd better deliver," he finally said.

They didn't know he meant it.

They returned to the game, and Lenny understood how far out he was. It was everything he wasn't ready for, yet there he was, fumbling and flailing and loving it. He scratched his head and hoped something came loose, like a plan.

The stakes were beyond him, and he was beyond confused.

They turned back to the cards. He was the wild card.

"Guess I've delivered worse!" Lenny thought, an underdog on a throne. He needed this delivery—more than they knew.

The game was tense, the cards shuffled like they were taunting Lenny. He was in too deep.

"Since our delivery guy hasn't shown," Olu said, turning his warmth businesslike attention to Lenny, "how would you like to make $250,000?"

"Hold on. Did my guy just say, $250,000?" Lenny blinked back

the thought. He thought of pizza, money, then pizza again. His brain scrambled. He could buy a thousand Tonys! He scratched his head.

Seeing Lenny lost in his thoughts, "And if you're thinking pizza, think again. You'll be delivering a briefcase, not pizza," Olu said, his voice gentle and precise.

Lenny nodded, his enthusiasm an untamed beast. "That's like twenty-five thousand large pepperonis!"

The others exchanged glances. Confusion was written on all their faces. It was impossible for someone like Lenny, but they had the money to risk it. And it could be fun.

The game grew silent as Lenny's mind mapped Baltimore. They watched, knowing him better than he knew himself.

He fidgeted with cards, the potential sum blinding in its improbability.

"The briefcase does not contain drugs," Olu stressed.

"Or anything illegal," Kim added. "We're above such trivial matters," she dismissed the idea with a flick of her wrist.

"Is everyone sure about this?" Ms. Khadijah al-Hari asked, her gaze still locked onto her cards.

"Oh, we do, Ms. Khadijah al-Hari," Olu said.

Their eyes bore into him, each second longer than the last, waiting to see if he'd fold or rise to the challenge.

Lenny's thoughts raced faster than his car. "That's like a billion small pizzas!" His mind was still locked on the possibilities.

They didn't know Tony called him the Baltimore Rabbit. Lenny's brain burst with visions of success. His hands shook with too much energy to control.

"It's almost enough to make me nervous," he said, grabbing confidence he didn't have.

Lenny calculated the money in his head, the numbers so big they scared him. "Is there a catch?" he asked, suspicion and excitement fighting for dominance.

"None," Olu assured, calm and composed.

The clock ticked. They wanted to see him sweat, and he did, but not enough to give up. They let him stew in the possibility, the room an echo chamber of anticipation.

He didn't believe it, but he wanted to. This was his break. He had to deliver.

They studied him, waiting. They knew the stakes. They didn't think he did.

Lenny wondered what Tony would say, probably something with more doubt and less risk. Heck, Tony would probably wish he had made this delivery himself.

"How can I say no?" he yelled, voice cracking with raw ambition. "This is bigger than extra-large!" He was in over his head, but that never stopped him before.

Lenny's optimism made him bold. He didn't have the brains to say no. He couldn't back out now.

"I'm your guy!" he declared, almost surprised at his own conviction.

They watched like scientists observing a lab rat on a suicide mission. They were impressed. He was insane.

The money sparkled like delivery dreams. It was more than rent; it was his life on a golden platter. Lenny loved those odds.

"Hope the briefcase tips!" he said, arms flailing.

"Only if the case remains closed," Saito said, finally breaking his silence.

They smiled, sly and knowing.

He wondered why.

The stakes were impossible. So was Lenny. His confidence

defied reason.

The cards shuffled again, a deck stacked against him. But he was all in, and he meant it.

The stakes crystallized as the players laid down bets. Slick Vic aligned his chips with robotic accuracy. "Fifty percent chance he makes it past the gate," he said.

Lenny scratched his head.

Khadijah doubled a side bet. "Does he cry or wet himself first?" she asked.

Lenny's eyes bulged. *"Cry...wet?"* He repeated in his head.

Kim tapped on her tablet. "His chances are slim," she noted. "Statistically speaking."

"I do hear you guys. And I'm the best delivery guy in the state," Lenny said with confidence.

The group brushed off his comments and pressed forward.

Olu pushed a massive stack in the center of the table. "That's what makes it fun!"

"Delivery has to be completed by morning," Slick Vic said, eyeing the others around the table.

Lenny grinned. "By morning? That's nothing! Tony times me on deliveries all the time."

The odds were against him, but he didn't care.

"Vic...where has your sense of the thrill gone?" Kim said with a smile that even made Lenny's skin prickle with something special.

Slick Vic meticulously aligned chips, measuring Lenny's resolve. The odds were long, but so were his chances.

"Past the gate," Vic calculated, as if predicting the weather.

"Maybe," said Khadijah, laughing. "If he's lucky."

Lenny shook his head, and more courage came loose. "I'm faster than I look," he assured, unaware of their doubts. "That's how I make rent."

The players regarded him as a wild gamble, all bets off and off the wall.

Khadijah provocatively raised a side bet, enjoying the game as much as the challenge. "He might make it," she conceded. "But sanity intact?"

She made him sweat. Kim tapped her tablet, eyes sparkling with a mix of curiosity and skepticism. "Slim odds," she said. "He could surprise us. Or just be a surprise."

They knew Lenny had no idea how crazy he was.

Olu placed a huge wager, and Lenny couldn't believe it. More than rent. More than the planet. He'd never been the center of such rich attention.

Mr. Saito gave a subtle nod, acknowledging Lenny like he was a piece on a chessboard.

Lenny's eyes were as big as his dreams. "My life's a gamble," he said, loving the thrill. "I'm your wild card!"

Lenny thought about rent, a new car, his own pizza show, and laughed at the stakes. They seemed bigger than his future, but he loved the ride. He scratched his head, smiling like he'd already won.

It was beyond crazy, and so was he.

"Can I get that in writing?" he asked, half serious, half wild. "Delivery guaranteed!"

They gave him an unreadable smile. The briefcase wasn't the only mystery. Lenny's optimism was another enigma.

They watched him sign his name on something that looked official, like a high-stakes contract or a ransom note. The millionaires watched him with an amused detachment, and he was thrilled to be the underdog in such an exclusive race.

Lenny loved those odds.

Olu bent down, his fingers brushing against the perfect carpet, and emerged with a gleaming stainless-steel briefcase. He set it down on the card table with a decisive thud. "Here we go," he declared, nudging the briefcase toward Lenny with a sly grin.

Taking hold of the briefcase, "Hampden route, twenty-eight minutes flat!" he bragged.

"I once did twenty-seven," Saito said, with a smile.

"A challenge, then. Count me in," Lenny grins, nodding enthusiastically.

The silence stretched, and then it was shattered by laughter. It filled the room, but Lenny felt like he was laughing hardest of all.

The odds were impossible, but Lenny didn't care. He shook on it, risking everything. His confidence defied reason, but it was the only thing he trusted.

"Better than pepperoni on a payday!"

Cryptic Cheesey Counsel

The mansion exhaled him, laughter trailing like expensive perfume. Lenny hugged the stainless-steel briefcase, life more impossible and thrilling with each step. His car lurked in the shadows, a trusty steed among a stable of luxury. He tossed the briefcase onto the seat, its thud a reminder that his optimism was untested at this moment. The whole world waited for this delivery, and he grinned. It wasn't just rent money; it was victory in a box. He could taste the payday, but right now, all he had was faith and pepperoni stains. He clung to both and gunned the engine.

Lenny raced into the night, his car hiccuping as it shot through the outskirts of Baltimore. His hands shook, the briefcase watching him like a wild animal, and the clock ticking louder than his muffler.

"Outrunning fear is a form of cardio!" he yelled, hoping his favorite self-help podcast would agree.

The GPS coughed up an intersection, but Lenny's gut said another thing. He chose instinct over technology, and the briefcase slid ominously across the seat.

The car felt more alive than ever, as if it knew the stakes were more than just pepperoni and cheese.

"Every opportunity's a gift," Lenny mumbled, wiping sweat

from his brow. "Unless it's ticking!" His laugh was half terror, half glee.

The GPS cut out with an indignant chirp, and Lenny glared at it like an old rival. He spun the wheel, tires screeching as he darted onto a shortcut that had once gotten him fired but had always been faster.

Pikesville loomed ahead, but he was racing more than the clock. He was racing doubt, bad odds, and his better judgment.

Lenny's grip on the wheel was white-knuckled and hopeful, the two things he did best. He ignored the GPS, ignored the rattles, ignored the tiny voice in his head that sounded a lot like Tony, warning him he'd bite off more than he could chew. But chewing big was Lenny's style.

"The biggest risks have the cheesiest rewards!" he muttered, convinced he could taste success.

He could practically see Uncle Red's chaotic world from here, just as convoluted and inscrutable as the man himself. It was a beacon and a warning sign, all rolled into one, but Lenny didn't care. The road stretched before him, and he leaned into the chaos.

He took a wild turn, heart pounding, as his sweat formed a small creek down his neck. The thrill of it all, the uncertainty, the manic, pizza-fueled optimism—it was intoxicating.

The delivery game had never been higher. Lenny wouldn't have it any other way.

The GPS blinked back to life just as he pulled into a narrow street, mocking him with directions he'd already known. He laughed, a sound of pure, nervous triumph. This was it, and Lenny was more in the game than he'd ever been in his life.

His foot barely hit the brake as he arrived. Uncle Red's townhouse stood defiantly amidst the quieter Pikesville landscape, a clash of colors and conspiracies. Lenny parked haphazardly, the briefcase a heavy promise at his side.

He took a deep breath, the cool night air mixing with his frantic heartbeat. The mission was alive, like him, like his car, and he grinned at the thrill of it all. This was more than a delivery; it was everything.

The briefcase felt as though it weighed a million pounds as Lenny hauled it up the front steps. He was breathless, but that might have been nerves or the dusting of paranoia in the air. Uncle Red's townhouse stood out from amongst the rest, a secretive grandeur, colors too bright for Pikesville and sanity.

Lenny mashed the doorbell, and it sounded like a typewriter from a bad detective novel. He braced himself for the peculiar, incense-scented universe beyond the door. It swung open, as if on cue, and there was Uncle Red—a festive spy in a velvet tracksuit. His grin was conspiratorial with a fake Belgian mustache wide enough to hide the secrets of the universe.

Lenny hesitated for a second, feeling like he'd landed in the middle of an epic conspiracy. His instincts said to run, but his commitment shouted louder. The promise of $250,000 gave him courage. He wanted to make sure he was doing the best thing. He took a step inside.

The townhouse was an explosion of sensory overload. Bright and jarring, it defied logic with its wild décor and strange gadgets. A chandelier made of mismatched light bulbs flickered, casting dizzying patterns on walls lined with dusty electronics. It was like a scene from a retro spy movie, except all the extras had quit and taken their scripts with them. The air was heavy with incense, almost a living thing that threatened to wrap itself around Lenny and pull him into Uncle Red's universe.

It was impossible to tell if the place was meticulously designed chaos or just chaos. Lenny's head spun as he tried to make sense of it all.

Uncle Red's laughter was a symphony of madness, echoing through the rooms. "The delivery boy seeks wisdom!" he declared, more delighted than surprised. "Oh, and it's good to see my boy," he continued, as he gave him a strong pat on the shoulder.

Lenny stumbled over his words, the energy of the place seeping into him. "Uncle Red, I—"

"Don't tell me!" Uncle Red interrupted, his eyes glinting like he'd already pieced together the entire story. "The ghost ship runs aground! The pigeon finds its coop!" He looked at the briefcase with a mixture of amusement and suspicion.

"Yeah, I guess you could say that," Lenny said, knowing he was already swept up in the madness, more excited than confused, which was a rare treat for him.

"The universe sends you to me with a bounty, and you're wondering if it's the truth or just another mirage in the desert of existence!" Uncle Red's grin widened, if that was possible. "You're right to be suspicious."

Lenny followed him deeper into the chaos, feeling like he'd stepped into another world. He wasn't sure if he loved it or feared it. Probably both.

Uncle Red bounced around like a kid in a candy store, only the candy was surveillance equipment and things that went beep in the night. He wore an outfit so bright it could probably be seen from space, mismatched sneakers adding to the ensemble. An oversized fake mustache completed the look, threatening to slip off with each animated movement.

Lenny felt like he was in a living fever dream. It was brilliant, terrifying, and incredibly Uncle Red.

"So, Lenny!" Uncle Red exclaimed, rubbing his hands together. "The last time I saw a look like that, a seal was playing cards with the CIA!"

Lenny stood there, feeling like the floor might eat him. "This poker game," he said, trying to make it sound like he knew what he was talking about. "They want me to deliver this."

He held up the briefcase like it was an unexploded bomb. Uncle Red's gaze was electric, filled with the kind of intensity that suggested he might see through walls, time, and bad delivery scams.

"The trap is set! And the moon is ago!" Uncle Red announced, poking at the briefcase with exaggerated caution. "The question is: Are you the cat or the mouse?" His laughter filled the room again, a joyful noise that made Lenny grin despite himself.

"I think I'm just the guy in the wrong place," Lenny said, though he wasn't entirely sure he meant it. "I'm supposed to take it to Hampden."

"The universe plays a dangerous game," Uncle Red mused, nodding like he had nothing but time and ten thousand theories. "But you are bold, young Bruno! Bold and perhaps a bit saucy!" His eyes darted between Lenny and the corners of the room.

Lenny turned to see what Uncle Red was staring at, but all he could make out were shadows that danced and flickered under the erratic glow of the strobing lights, twisting as if they had a life of their own.

"Is that a mild, tangy, or spicy sauce, Uncle Red?" Lenny asked as he tried to follow the logic, but it was like chasing a runaway cheese wheel. "So, you think it's a bad idea?" He couldn't keep the disappointment out of his voice, even though he knew the answer.

"I think," Uncle Red said, suddenly serious, "it's the best

kind of bad idea. And the worst kind of good one!"

They both looked at the briefcase, then at each other, and burst into laughter. Inappropriate and too loud, it bounced off the walls and made everything feel strangely perfect.

Uncle Red stepped closer, "Sit down, the briefcase son and give me your hands," he leaned in, his breath warming Lenny's face, carrying a faint whiff of bourbon with a hint of cheese, and not just any cheese but asiago.

Lenny's bones buzz with an odd thrill as he sets the briefcase down on the floor, his hands extending outward like he's about to unveil a magic trick.

Uncle Red clasped Lenny's hands, spreading his fingers wide, peering into the creases and lines as if he were deciphering a cosmic map etched in flesh.

"Oh, this is going to be the most difficult challenge you have ever come to face," he began, his face etched with seriousness. "Like catching a monkey washing a cat, it will be. And seeing that, is finding gold at the end of the rainbow."

"I'm I the cat or the—"

"Shhh," Uncle Red demanded, maintaining his focus. He paused as if choosing his next words carefully, "The sky's little eye will buzz like a hornet hungry for cheese," he cackles. "A bearded goat will demand its due when the moon is highest!" he continued, his fake mustache slipping slightly. "You'll roll with others to get soaked by suds you never ordered, but that's how the universe rinses away doubt!" He finally finished, letting go of Lenny's hand and clasping his own together with a sense of reverence.

Lenny freezes for a heartbeat, caught off guard by Uncle Red's sudden stillness. His hands clasped together as if in fervent prayer, Uncle Red's silence hangs heavy in the air. Confusion swirls in Lenny's mind as he takes in the scene, his eyes darting around the cluttered room, searching for clues to decipher this unexpected moment. The place was filled with odd devices, and the smell of incense was overpowering. It was a world unto itself, a circus of possibilities that left Lenny feeling dizzy and more alive than he'd ever been.

"Now about all you—"

Immediately, Uncle Red's eyes opened as he snapped to his senses, "That's all I got for you, son. The universe can only give what exists," he said, prompting Lenny towards the front door. "Now you must go before the CIA thinks you're from the beyond," opening the front door with haste.

"Thank you, Uncle R—"

The door banged shut, cutting off his words like a knife.

Lenny pivoted sharply, his mismatched delivery uniform rustling as he strode toward his car, determination etched across his face. Getting into the driver's seat, he didn't know if he was getting what he came for, but he was getting something.

Maybe the wild ride of his life.

Prepping for the Pepperonies

Lenny, now back in his car, pushed the vehicle hard along the interstate. He mashed the gas, rolling down his window and cranking the heat to dry the cold sweat that kept leaking from his forehead. The stainless-steel briefcase in the passenger seat loomed in the dashboard's flicker, as menacing as a loaded mousetrap.

He eyed it every few seconds, half-expecting the thing to grow teeth or a mouth and start critiquing his driving. The air in the car vibrated with a funk equal parts garlic, anxiety, and the overworked engine. Every time he crested a pothole, the briefcase bounced and thunked against the seat like it wanted to break free. The pizza-slice bobblehead on the dash twitched and spasmed, nodding at every bad decision.

Somewhere between a defunct Checkers and a strip-mall dentist, his phone began to vibrate. The screen glared: TONY. In all caps, as if Tony Martinelli had hacked the caller ID just to yell at people. Lenny's heart went into full popcorn mode.

"Aw, geez, Lenny. How could I forget?" he mused internally.

He considered letting it ring out. But Tony was the kind of guy who believed missed calls were a sign of moral weakness, like not tipping or eating frozen pizza. He snatched the phone, thumbed it to speaker, and braced for impact.

"Bruno. Where the hell are you?"

Lenny's free hand death-gripped the wheel, knuckles bone-white. "Hey, Tony! I'm, uh—on my way. Traffic is murder out here. Swear on my parole officer's life."

"You're not on parole, you idiot. You're forty and you still deliver pizza. What's the holdup, Bruno?" Tony barked over the speaker.

He tried to sound casual, like he wasn't sweating through two layers of polyester uniform. "So, funny story," he said, glancing at the briefcase and wondering if it counted as an accomplice, "See what had happened was—the city's got this— like, a sinkhole? It ate a whole building right in front of me. Not a big building, just one of those, uh, historical row houses."

There was a pause so thick you could spread it on a bagel.

"A whole sinkhole," Tony said dryly.

"Yeah, just opened up and woosh, gone. Bricks everywhere. I'm rerouting," Lenny explained.

Tony sighed, a sound like cheese grating against its will. "You want to explain how a sinkhole only affects you? Everybody else made it back. Heck, even DeShawn, and he drives like he's allergic to acceleration."

Lenny's mind raced. "I think it was a, uh, targeted sinkhole. The city's after me, Tony. You've seen my parking tickets?"

"Cute." Tony's tone could curdle milk. "Well, I've got an address in Ashburton waiting on a delivery, and if you're not back in twenty, I'm docking tips for the week."

"C'mon, Tony, a week?"

"Probably two if we keep this absurd story up," Tony said, a hint of frustration in his voice.

"No problem, deliveries guaranteed," Lenny said, voice cracked and desperate for moisture. He jerked the wheel to avoid a manhole cover, "Not that there'll be a week if this goes wrong," he muttered as he checked the rearview mirror for the fourth time in thirty seconds.

"You know, I had you down for this big delivery for an overnight party. Twenty pizzas minimum," Tony said, in an attempt to goad Lenny on.

"Twenty?"

"Yeah, twenty. And you know, an order that large has a tip included at eighteen percent. So are you going to make it back here in the next fifteen to twenty," Tony asked.

Lenny's mind whirred in a momentary stillness, the weight of the offer hanging in the air like an overcooked pizza on a hot summer day. And he almost said yes. He almost abandoned the briefcase, the high-stakes madness, the quarter-million-dollar payday, for a chance to prove he wasn't just the biggest screw-up on Tony's payroll. But then he saw the way the light glinted off the briefcase, like it was trying to signal him. He thought of rent. Of Tony's threats. Of every motivational tape and every time he'd ever said yes when he should have said hell no.

"Actually, Tony, I gotta, uh, make a call first. There's a— family situation. Urgent. You said once family came first, right?"

There was another pause, and Lenny could almost see Tony rolling his eyes, with his eyes locked on the clock.

"Fifteen minutes, Bruno. After that, I get someone else to deliver, and you're out a week's pay."

"It might be best if you just get someone else on it, this sinkhole ain't moving," Lenny continued.

"You know what, Bruno-"

The call ended before Lenny could respond.

With the call dropped, Lenny continued driving, frequently glancing at the address for the briefcase delivery.

"This better be worth skipping out on twenty pizzas," Lenny muttered to himself, exhaling a heavy sigh that echoed his frustration.

He took a deep breath and floored it, tires shrieking as he lurched forward on the highway. He barely heard the sound of his phone ringing again—Tony, of course—but he let it go to voicemail this time. He was done with pizza, done with excuses, done with being the underdog who never bet on himself.

The highway lights blurred past, flickering, as they went, as if they were mocking him. His hands still trembled, but this time it was with something dangerously close to hope. The briefcase sat heavy in the passenger seat, a promise of something new.

"Screw you lights, this is my world. This is my chance," he yelled out the window, in the darkness.

He pulled off onto the next exit, a shortcut to his destination. The world shrank to nothing but the sound of his breath and the thump of his heart upon a lone road.

He whispered to himself, "No more setbacks. Time to deliver."

And for once, Lenny Bruno believed it.

The Goat Who Stole Christmas

Lenny rocketed up the back roads of Baltimore County with the windows cracked, as if the extra oxygen could outpace the pounding of his heart. The city had picked up a cool summer breeze beneath the full moon, broken only by his car's jaundiced headlights and the erratic blinking of dashboard warning lights.

He was alone. The only other living soul was a bored deer on the shoulder, who raised its head in judgment as he screamed past, clinging to the wheel with one hand and the stainless-steel briefcase with the other. The briefcase sat in the passenger seat like a well-behaved mafia enforcer, silent but threatening.

Lenny's mind looped with visions of tomorrow: Rent paid, a new set of tires, maybe even take some time off from work. The future was hot, fresh, and just a little burnt at the edges. Just the way he liked it.

The car coughed. Then again, but deeper, like a smoker's last Christmas. The engine rumbled and cut. The motivational podcast died mid-pep talk, its words lost in static as he pulled off to the side of the road. The headlights dimmed, then surrendered completely. In an instant, Lenny was cocooned in black, the only illumination from the cheap phone mount on his dash.

He blinked. "No, no, no," he muttered, slapping the wheel

like it had personally insulted him. "You can't do this now. Not today!"

He jiggled the key. The engine clicked, then let out a whine like an old man denied a Social Security check. Lenny slammed the hood release and threw himself out into the night.

Outside, the world was all cool and silent, a sort of cosmic waiting room. Lenny stomped to the hood, trailing the scent of oregano and desperation. He yanked it open, squinting into the darkness. The engine looked the same as always: a hunk of metal, hoses, and weird green fluid he pretended was supposed to be there. He poked at things, hoping the car would sense his confidence.

"Alright, automotive gods," he muttered, "what's your sacrifice policy?" He said before he offered a crusty gum wrapper to the night, then gripped the edge of the hood and gave it a motivational slam.

Nothing. The engine sat inert, unimpressed.

Feeling that he still had to do something, Lenny made his way to the trunk, his sneakers crunching on loose gravel as he flung it open. Inside, a chaotic jumble of pizza boxes teetered next to half-empty coolant bottles, their labels faded and sticky. His fingers fished through the clutter until they landed on a ratchet set, shiny but untouched. He held it up, squinting at the tools as if expecting them to sprout arms and start fixing his car for him. With a dramatic flair, he twisted a couple of bolts that sat exposed beneath the hood, pretending to know what he was doing before slamming the hood shut with a frustrated huff. He marched back to the driver's seat, his shoulders squared.

He tried the key again. The car shuddered, made a sound like a blender swallowing its own blades, then spat out a single, wheezing beep. All the lights—check engine, airbag, battery, possibly one that just said "ABANDON HOPE"—flared and faded.

Lenny dropped his head to the wheel. The tinsel on his hat scratched his ear. He wanted to scream. Instead, he whispered, "You gotta be kidding me."

There was no shoulder here, no traffic, just an endless field and the silhouette of woods. His phone battery blinked at him: 35%.

It was a walk or nothing.

He considered calling Tony. Or the millionaires. Or anyone who might send an Uber and not laugh at him for dying on the way to a quarter-million-dollar gig. But instead, he opened his phone, flicked on the flashlight, and clipped the briefcase shut with a sort of grim dignity.

He stepped out. The silence pressed in. No city noises. Just the hiss of summer's wind in the stalks and a distant, irregular crunch he hoped was deer and not an axe murderer.

He locked the car out of habit. Why? He wasn't sure. If anyone wanted to steal that heap, Lenny would've bought them lunch.

The walk started easily enough. He kept to the shoulder, moving at a brisk pace, every few steps glancing behind him as if the car might have a change of heart and follow. The moon came out in full, spotlighting the ribbon of asphalt ahead and turning his breath to little clouds. He walked, counting his steps.

"This isn't so bad. If I keep the pace, I'll be in Towson in no time, "he grumbled under his breath, trying to lift his spirits.

Half a mile in, the world got quieter. No bugs. No cars. Just the squeak of his sneakers and the whisper of his own nervous mantra. He started humming a jingle from work, something about "hot deals all day and night," until he realized it was making him more anxious. He stopped. The woods were thicker here, trees bunching close to the road, their trunks black and angular like prison bars.

He fumbled the phone, adjusting the flashlight. Its beam cut a weak tunnel through the dark, bouncing off the reflective pizza logo on his shirt. He hugged the briefcase to his chest and quickened his pace, the chill now more than just weather.

That's when the scream came.

It started as a high whine, pitched beyond human but not quite animal, then modulated down to a guttural shriek, like someone had stepped on a baby and a tire iron at the same time. Lenny's spine locked. His feet planted. He spun, the flashlight swinging wild arcs through the trees, chasing shadows that never quite resolved into anything real.

He stood frozen, heart slamming in his chest. Then, another noise—a crunch, closer this time, in the underbrush just behind the guardrail.

"Hey!" he yelled, but his voice cracked, and the word was less a threat and more a confused yelp.

He shuffled backwards, flashlight trained on the thicket. He heard another rustle, then two glowing dots appeared, suspended in the black, like eyes on a Halloween prop. Lenny's brain, running on pure panic, did the math: too close to the ground for a person, too high for a raccoon, too symmetrical for comfort.

He fumbled his phone, almost dropped it, then stared again. The eyes blinked, then a snout jutted into the beam, long and bizarrely human in its expression. A pair of curling horns followed, then a shaggy, spectral shape, white as a cloud bank and just as insubstantial in the moonlight.

It was a goat. A big one, chewing on something.

"It's just a goat," he said, as he let out a nervous and pathetic laugh. "You gave me a heart attack, buddy." He made a shooing motion. "Go back to your field, pal. I got a job to do."

The goat did not shoo. It stepped onto the shoulder, eyes fixed on Lenny, head bobbing with an unblinking menace. Its hooves made a sharp clack on the blacktop, and every time it exhaled, a curl of vapor snorted out and drifted up, like the animal was vaping pure evil.

"Go," Lenny insisted, waving the briefcase at it. "Move. Find a can or something. Get back to your Bae," doing his best to mimic a sheep.

The goat didn't move. Instead, it lowered its head, horns shining in the moonlight, and let out another scream. It was louder this time. Closer. Lenny's relief evaporated, replaced with a cold, animal terror.

The goat charged.

Lenny's brain tried to process: Was this normal? Did goats do this? Was this the legendary "Ram of Pikesville," or was he just about to be gored to death on a delivery of a lifetime?

He didn't wait to find out. Lenny spun on his heel and ran, briefcase clamped to his chest, the phone's flashlight dancing crazed spots in his path. He heard the clatter of hooves behind him, the goat's bleat now a battle cry. It sounded faster than it had any right to be. Lenny sprinted down the shoulder, already gasping for air, his knees buckling with every stride.

"Not today!" he yelled, half-mad. "You want the briefcase, take it up with management!"

The goat gained on him, the clatter of hooves impossibly loud. Lenny risked a look back—the animal was only yards away, horns lowered, eyes wild. He tried to zig-zag, but the thing was agile, sticking to his trail like glue.

He stepped into a pothole full of water, stumbled, and barely kept upright. The goat missed his leg by a hair, but Lenny swore he felt the brush of fur and the chill of animal intent. He ran harder, lungs on fire, feet numb. The pizza hat flew off, lost to the night. He didn't care. All that mattered was staying ahead, making it to the next intersection, the next milestone, the next breath.

The goat screamed again, close enough to touch.

Lenny screamed right back, a sound so undignified it would haunt him for years. But he didn't stop. He kept moving, every stride powered by pure, high-grade terror.

He was alive. For now.

But the goat was alive as well and gaining.

Lenny's feet slapped the frozen asphalt, every stride a lunge into uncertainty. The night wrapped tighter, branches arching over the road in black arches, funneling him straight into doom. He risked a backward glance; the goat was closer now, jaws working, eyes two cold lanterns of intent. He tried to outpace it with pure will, but his legs were already flagging, the adrenaline spike crashing down to a sugary panic.

He vaulted the guardrail without thinking, tinsel hat long gone, landing in the weeds with the grace of a half-thawed chicken. The briefcase almost slipped from his grip, but Lenny wrestled it back, as if letting go would mean more than his own life. The goat's hooves rapped over the guardrail, and it skidded after him, a four-legged missile with no quit in its DNA.

He barreled through brambles, their thorns catching his pizza uniform and turning it into a tear-away tracksuit. Mud sucked at his sneakers, every step a gamble. The woods came alive with the goat's hellish shriek and the wet slap of Lenny's panicked flight.

"Okay, okay!" he shouted, as if this were a customer complaint he could defuse. "You want half a pizza? Extra cheese—capisce? Half off! Anything you want, pal!"

He ducked under a low limb, the goat nearly clipping his heels. He twisted left, lost his balance, and slammed shoulder-first into a rotten log. Spongy fungus burst in a spray of spores. Lenny sneezed, coughed, and realized he was already crawling on hands, knees, and the slippery side of desperation.

The woods thinned, moonlight picking out a faint trail ahead. There was bright light ahead, civilization. Lenny scrambled forward, shoes barely making purchase on the leaf-slime. The goat nipped at his heels, ripping a line up the back of his pants that would have mortified him if he weren't about to die. He rolled, came up staggering, and pivoted to put a sapling between himself and his pursuer.

The goat circled. Lenny fumbled with the briefcase, wielding it like a shield. "You wanna talk about this, maybe? I know a great place that does goat-friendly toppings! Very progressive. Gluten-free crust!" He swung the briefcase as the goat feinted, barely missing a horn to the ribs.

The goat screamed again, louder than before. Lenny, not to be outdone, screamed right back—his, a raw-throated delivery driver's ululation, spiking into a register only dogs (and now goats) could hear. The stand-off stretched for a breathless moment, neither party blinking.

Lenny did what he always did when backed into a corner: improvise. He chucked the briefcase up the hill, then bolted after it, using the distraction to gain a few precious yards. The goat, apparently the world's only certified briefcase specialist, followed. Lenny scooped the thing up mid-stride and, with the goat right on him, crashed through a final line of brush and into blinding electric daylight.

He careened into a parking lot dazzling with Christmas lights. Rows of blue spruce and noble fir were stacked like artillery, each festooned with a full arsenal of ornaments. The air snapped with pine and hot plastic. Sleigh bell music blasted from hidden speakers.

He tripped over a string of blinking lights and landed face-first into a display of tinsel garland. The briefcase skidded away and stopped at the foot of a plywood cut-out of the baby Jesus. For one weird second, Lenny thought he'd died and gone to a holiday-themed afterlife.

The goat burst from the shadows of the trees, eyes wide and bewildered as it took in the festive scene. It let out a low, skeptical snort, then readied itself for another charge. Lenny didn't stick around to find out what that might entail. He scuttled sideways like a crab toward the briefcase, his hands trembling like jelly on a rollercoaster.

Without a second thought, he seized the nearest Christmas tree—its branches fluffed up like an overzealous hairdo—and hoisted it as if it were a shield in some bizarre holiday battle. To his surprise, the tree was feather-light and came along willingly, trailing behind him like a glittery banner adorned with tinsel, faux snowflakes, and an assortment of discount ornaments that jingled cheerfully with every hurried step.

As he backed away, the goat charged again. Lenny held the tree like a lion-tamer's chair. The goat crashed headlong into the branches, showering the lot with glass balls and silver icicles, but the tree absorbed most of the hit, collapsing over the goat and pinning it for a crucial two seconds.

"You want a tree? Take it!" Lenny shrieked, hoping the animal understood the holiday spirit.

The commotion finally brought human intervention. From the shadow of a shipping container, a burly man in a red flannel jacket (one sleeve missing, revealing a tattooed arm that could have been a ham hock) came roaring onto the scene. He wore a Santa hat stapled to his head, beard stained with the memory of many peppermint schnapps. His eyes zeroed in on Lenny, then the goat, then the trashed tree display.

"What the hell are you doing to my Christmas trees, boy?" the man bellowed, voice so deep it even rattled the goat. He pointed a pruning saw at Lenny and started toward him with murder in his stride.

Lenny panicked. He yanked the tree upright, ornaments tinkling like wind chimes, and wedged himself behind it. "It's not what it looks like! I was—I was being chased!"

The goat, having extracted itself from the tree, let out a warble of triumph and bounded forward. The lot owner, seeing the goat, did a double-take.

"Oh, not again," he muttered, lowering the saw. "Goddamn Blitzen. That's the third time this week."

The goat, undeterred, banged horns against the side of the shipping container and then turned its attention back to Lenny, who was now wedged between a display of inflatable snowmen and a discounted wreath bin. He tried to sidestep, but the man advanced.

"Put the tree down and get off my lot!" the owner thundered.

"I'm trying!" Lenny yelled. He shook the tree, but it snagged on his pizza shirt, and for a moment, man and tree were fused into a lurching tangle of panic and plaid. The goat bleated, flared its nostrils, and advanced again.

"You selling these things or training them for the Kentucky Derby?" Lenny hollered, half-hysterical.

The owner hesitated, weighing the relative threat of Lenny vs. the goat, then made his call. "Drop the tree and scram! Or I call the cops, and you can explain why you're assaulting livestock!"

The goat made another rush. Lenny juked, tree and all, but the animal was quicker; it butted him square in the hip, sending him rushing out onto the neighboring road.

Like a sprinter in the final lap of a night track meet, Lenny dashed down the center of the road, one hand clutching the mysterious briefcase while the other awkwardly balanced the small Christmas tree. Hot on his heels were his two relentless pursuers, closing in with every frantic step he took.

"It's summertime! Why are you selling Christmas trees anyway?" Lenny yelled, managing to take a glance without falling. "What do you want from me?"

The goat lets out another ear-splitting bleat while the man glares at him, barking back, "Either pay up or return my tree!"

Turn a bend in the road, a faint, blue-tinted glow shimmered up ahead. Lenny squinted, for a second convinced he was hallucinating. But no, it was real—a suburban playground, weirdly well-lit for this hour, a cast of empty swings and jungle gym shadows stretching out in the frost. It looked both welcoming and haunted, the kind of place where people went to score illicit substances or, in Lenny's case, to hide from farm animals with an axe to grind.

He staggered toward the playground, every few steps glancing over his shoulder for signs of goat activity. The Christmas tree he'd grabbed in the melee was still clamped in his fist, and he only now noticed he'd been dragging it for half a block. He tried to toss it aside in a flourish, but the branches caught on his sleeve, nearly yanking him off balance. He did a one-legged hop, spun, and finally flung the tree into a picnic table, shattering a couple of red bulbs.

The playground loomed, with its plastic fortresses and unearthly-colored tube slides. Lenny's breath fogged ahead of him, making halos in the blue light. He picked the tallest slide—a garish orange spiral—and hustled toward it, the briefcase threatening to slip from his sweaty fingers. At the base, he clambered inside, wedging himself halfway up, back pressed against the curved wall, and tried to breathe quietly. The plastic smelled faintly of disinfectant and old gum, but it was warm, almost cozy. He hugged the briefcase to his chest and tried to control the trembling in his hands.

His mind spun out of control as he tried to figure out what was happening. The adrenaline and sweat stinging his eyes and fear made it hard to track reality. What was it in this case that was worth nearly getting killed by an animal? Why were the rich people so interested in him—Lenny Bruno, failed pizza mogul and part-time joke? Why were goats now part of the plot? He didn't know, and for once, he didn't have a theory.

He waited, listening. For a few minutes, there was only the gentle whir of the playground lights, the distant rumble of a highway, and his own heart punching a tattoo against his ribs.

Then, muffled footsteps. Not hoof beats. Shoes.

He froze, pressing his nose to a small peephole in the slide. The glow from the playground lights created a stage, and onto it stepped the Christmas tree lot owner—red flannel, missing sleeve, and all. Right behind him was the goat, no Blitzen, now strangely calm, following the man like a well-trained dog.

They stopped under a streetlamp, directly in Lenny's line of sight. The man glanced around, hands on his hips. The goat did the same, scanning the shadows, almost as if they were both security guards working the late shift.

Lenny's brain short-circuited. "What in the world is this?" he whispered, mouth pressed against the briefcase's cold handle. He was genuinely afraid they'd hear him.

The man and goat seemed to communicate, not in words, but in something more primal. The man squatted and rubbed the goat's head. The goat let out a long, satisfied bleat. They stared at each other for a second, then both looked straight at the slide where Lenny was hiding.

He ducked back, flattening himself against the curve, praying to all known pizza gods that they hadn't spotted him. His chest went still, breath stopped, as he waited for the sound of the goat's hooves on the tube plastic. But nothing came. He counted to thirty, sweat running down the back of his neck. Then, slowly, he peeked out again.

The man and the goat were standing shoulder to shoulder, looking up at the moon like two old buddies sharing a smoke. The man nodded, as if coming to a conclusion, then patted the goat on the rump. Without a word, they turned and walked away, disappearing into the darkness around the bend.

Lenny waited. And waited. After five long minutes, he finally let his legs uncurl. He crawled to the end of the slide, stuck his head out, and looked both ways. The playground was empty. The coast was clear.

He slid down the last stretch, legs shaking, and collapsed at the base. He drew in long, sharp breaths, the cool air filling his lungs. He took stock of his body: pizza uniform shredded, arms scraped and sticky with tree sap, one shoe covered in mud, but otherwise intact. He checked the briefcase—no dents, the latch still sealed, still ticking, metaphorically or otherwise.

He checked the time on his cell phone: nearly two in the morning. He was hours behind schedule. He should have been at this destination by now.

He forced himself to his feet, scanned the playground one more time, and started walking. Each step was heavy, but lighter than before. He was alive. He had the goods. He was going to finish this delivery, no matter what.

Drone Wars

Lenny hadn't seen so many people vertical at two a.m. since his last mandatory staff meeting at Tony's, and even that was just six sleep-deprived drivers and one gluten-intolerant manager. Here, under the floodlights of Towson's shopping drag, it was a bender's finish line. The neon horde spilled from every bar, ice cream shop, and closed-out vape kiosk, a living river of college kids, ex-college kids, and people who looked like they'd never left the county since the Clinton administration.

Lenny limped along the sidewalk, drinking a Slurpee to quench his thirst, while cradling the gleaming briefcase like it was a gift for a loan shark. The adrenaline from his woodland jog had been replaced by the cold dread of civilization. His phone buzzed against his hip, and he slapped at it without breaking stride, but the screen flashed a cryptic number, not Tony, not anyone in his five "Favorites." The briefcase thumped against his thigh with each stride, heavy enough to remind him why his left kneecap ached. The further he walked, the more the city's noise settled into a kind of low, electrical hum, and he almost let himself believe he could disappear into the crowd.

Until he heard the buzzing.

It started as a mosquito, then graduated to a bumblebee, then to a cordless drill. Lenny looked up, squinting through streetlamp glare and the haze of vape clouds. There, above the intersection, hung a drone. Little, white, four-rotor, with a blinking red eye like a caffeinated R2-D2. It hovered, then dipped, then arced back up, making small, uncertain figure-eights over his head.

Lenny quickened his pace. The drone kept up.

He ducked his chin and plunged into the next knot of partiers. They were a bachelor party, all wearing matching shirts that read "I'M THE PROBLEM." He envied their group solidarity and lack of existential threat. Lenny tried to blend in, shuffling behind the tallest one, but the drone dipped lower, training its lens on him and holding there like an insult.

"Is that thing following you?" asked a woman with glitter under her eyes, holding a margarita the size of a fish tank.

"Lady, I'm not sure...But I think so," Lenny muttered, in a vain attempt to use her as a human shield.

The woman made a face, somewhere between amusement and horror. "Creepy," she said, and then to her friend: "That guy's got a drone stalker!"

A ripple of laughter moved through the group, and Lenny caught the phrase "Deliver us from evil," which would've stung if he hadn't already heard every pizza pun in existence. He lurched forward, past a squabble over Lyft fares, into the next storefront alcove.

"C'mon, the day is weird enough," he said with a whisper.

The drone didn't blink. It kept just overhead, tracking him with supernatural confidence, as if its pilot had spent hours learning the ballet of his walk cycle.

"This delivery's getting extra spicy," he mumbled, and ducked behind the oversized planters outside a sushi place. He pressed his back into the cold ceramic, the briefcase wedged between his knees, and peeked upward. The drone hovered just above, the red light pulsing like a countdown.

"No tip is worth this kind of heat," he thought.

There was nothing for it but to run. Lenny checked both ways, then sprinted across the crosswalk, nearly colliding with a couple in matching cargo shorts and a man in a bicycle helmet walking two Pomeranians. The dogs barked at the drone; the man barked at Lenny.

"Buddy! You got a license for that thing?" the man shouted, shaking a gloved fist.

"Not even for my car!" Lenny called back, already diving behind a newspaper vending box. He crouched there, breath coming in high, wheezy pants, trying to make himself as small as possible.

The drone, the little shit, adjusted altitude and trained its lens down through the warped plexiglass of the vending box. Lenny glared back, raised a middle finger, then darted out and straight into a crowd of lacrosse bros doing Jäger shots in the median.

The smell of Red Bull and man-sweat was a blanket. Lenny wriggled through them, keeping the briefcase under his armpit. Above, the drone's red eye bounced between streetlights and wires, never losing him.

He veered down a side alley, past the back doors of a brewery, and slid behind a dumpster overflowing with boxes and old food. The air was cool and sour. He pressed himself against the bricks and tried to steady his breathing.

It was then he heard, faint but clear, the voice.

"...all units, targets in quadrant three. Repeat, target in quadrant three, heading east on York—"

Lenny's spine went electric. The drone had a speaker, and

someone was on the other end, narrating his life like a bad action movie. He looked up, saw the drone hanging like a disapproving mother-in-law over the lip of the roof.

"What, are you the NSA? Get a real job!" Lenny shouted, before realizing he'd just blown his own cover to a literal robot.

A sliding door banged open, and two servers came out, cigarettes already lit, oblivious to the drama above. Lenny tried to act casual, sidling up to them.

"Hey, uh, weird question—how do you guys feel about... robots?" he said, as if it was a standard small talk opener.

One server—nose ring, half-lidded, maybe twenty—shrugged. "They're cool, I guess, as long as they don't take my tips."

"How about one that's recording you?" Lenny continued, pointing upward at the drone.

The other server, more awake, squinted at the drone. "Is that legal?" she asked.

"Define 'legal,'" Lenny said, and in one motion, bolted down the alley, servers gawping after him.

The next block was a blur of chain restaurant patios and roving packs of undergrads. Lenny used a group of drunk girls as cover, sliding into their photo op at just the right moment. The drone paused, confused by the sudden influx of identical-looking young people. Lenny smiled, put an arm around a stranger, and flashed a peace sign for the photo.

"You're in the shot, man!" one of them squealed.

"I live for the shot," Lenny said, then slid away, letting the crowd swallow him.

He rounded a corner and almost lost his balance, but kept his grip on the briefcase. The drone, regaining its bearings, swooped overhead, now barely twenty feet above his head.

"Persistent little bugger," Lenny muttered.

He ducked into the covered entrance of a 24-hour gym, plastered with posters promising "No Judgment" and "You're Your Only Competition." He collapsed on a bench, hunched over the case, and did his best to look like just another guy waiting for his Uber. A couple of fitness die-hards side-eyed him, but went back to arguing about protein shakes.

The drone hovered at the threshold, red eye unwavering. Lenny considered charging the doors and trying to lose it in the weight room, but figured that if the local gym rats were as persistent as this drone, he'd be bench pressing his own body weight by dawn.

He waited. The drone waited. For a few tense minutes, it was a standoff.

Then, the drone's eye flickered, and it slowly retreated up the block, rising until it was barely a speck against the sodium lights.

Lenny didn't trust it, not for a second. He rose, knees popping, and staggered out the opposite exit, keeping to the shadows, hurrying through the strip mall parking lot. He did his best to control his breathing. He checked the briefcase—still secure, still heavy as guilt.

He cut through a line of parked cars, weaving between hoods and mirrors, glancing upward every few steps. The drone didn't reappear. He started to relax, even let himself daydream for a minute, maybe two. Then a shriek of laughter from some passing party-goers startled him out of reverie. He ducked, tried to play it cool, but they'd already noticed him.

"Hey pizza guy!" one of them called, brandishing a tiara with little flashing LED stars. "You doing a delivery or just stalking us?"

"Just chasing my dreams, ma'am," Lenny replied, mustering his best customer service voice.

"Appears you're the one being chased!" another one pointed up.

He glanced skyward. There it was, again, the drone, this time with a blue LED blinking furiously.

"Love to continue chatting, ladies, but I gotta go," Lenny said, then bolted.

This time, Lenny doesn't waste a second on hiding. He sprints forward, legs thrumming like pistons, his breath coming in ragged gasps. The drone darts behind him, swooping lower and sending a mechanical buzz that vibrates against his eardrums. He veers toward the next alley, leaps over a rainwater puddle, skids on a slick patch of spilled fries that sends him momentarily off-balance, but he recovers and keeps going. As he races past a couple locked in an embrace on a loading dock, they break apart with wide eyes and shout encouragements, their cheers mingling with the chaos around him.

"Go, pizza man, go!" some guy yelled, fist-pumping.

He hit the end of the block, found himself boxed in by a fence. He spun, nearly slipping, as the drone hovered a few feet from his nose.

Lenny stared at it, sweat streaming down his face. For a second, it seemed to study him, the red eye and blue LED both blinking.

He did what any rational human would do. He stuck out his tongue and shouted, "You want a piece of me? I fold better than this crust! Just asked the goat that tried me."

It was pure reflex, but it felt good.

The drone beeped, then, as if sated, zipped up and away, disappearing behind the corner of the Chase Bank building.

Lenny slumped against the fence, hands shaking.

"That's right. Who's the doughboy now?" he said, though there was no one around to hear it.

He checked the sky. Clear. For now.

He checked his phone—27% battery and dropping, probably the drone's fault.

He checked the briefcase, still locked, still cold against his chest.

Hearing some commotion in the distance, he took a shaky breath, wiped his face, straightened up, and headed off.

—

It wasn't long before Lenny found the source of the sounds. If there was one thing he knew about the greater Towson area, it was that every parking structure doubled as a skate park after midnight. He'd delivered pies to half the kids who haunted them, and once, back when he thought he had a shot with "urban youth marketing," even tried to bribe a squad of longboarders into becoming viral street promoters for the pizzeria. That had ended in a spray-paint incident and two weeks of unpaid deliveries, but the point was: he knew the sound of urethane wheels on concrete.

Which is how, limping through the crisp neon of the strip mall, Lenny found himself drawn by instinct and a faint hope for sanctuary to the concrete bowl tucked behind the defunct Circuit City. Even from a block away, he could hear the pop-crack of kick-flips and the rolling, echoing taunt of "dude, you eat it again?" followed by the slapping of palms and the ritual hooting of teens left unsupervised for generations.

The skate park was lit by a single flickering halogen, which gave the whole scene the flavor of a Soviet interrogation room. Four kids owned the place: one in a NASA hoodie, two in matching Orioles hats, and the fourth—a girl, small, fast, with purple hair—was already halfway up the quarter pipe by the time Lenny hobbled into view.

He ducked into the shadow of the ramp, massaging his knee and pretending to check his phone. The briefcase, now decorated with a fat sticker reading "PROVE IT," dug into his ribs. For a second, it almost felt like he was back in high school, loitering where he shouldn't, waiting to get called out by someone with actual self-esteem.

The smallest kid, maybe fourteen, eyed him with full sub-urban suspicion. "Yo, what's with the fit?" He gestured at Lenny's mismatched pizza regalia with a flick of his chin.

"Uniform," Lenny said, forcing a smile. "It's, uh, retro." He scanned the sky. The drone wasn't in line of sight, but he'd seen enough to know it could pop up at any second.

The tallest skater—Orioles Hat #1—snorted. "You on some weird delivery service or what?"

"Nah, man," Lenny said, "I'm off the clock. Just, you know, passing through."

Purple Hair rolled up next to him, board clacking the curb. "Passing through with a briefcase? In the middle of the night? That's the creepiest thing I've seen since the Chick-fil-A cow took a dump in the ball pit."

Lenny held up the case. "It's not what you think."

Orioles Hat #2: "I'm thinking it's a bomb."

"Or porn," NASA Hoodie added, face deadpan. "Dude, please say it's porn."

Lenny barked a laugh, surprising even himself. "Not even close. It's, uh, more like... evidence. Of a crime I didn't commit."

He looked around, aware that the pitch was spiraling. "Look, I just need a place to hide. For, like, a minute. If anyone asks, you never saw me."

Purple Hair exchanged glances with the crew, then looked Lenny up and down, smirking. "We don't do narc work for free. Gotta earn it."

"Yeah," piped NASA Hoodie. "Show us a trick. Or at least don't biff it on the mini-ramp."

Lenny stared at them, then at the battered line of loaner boards stacked against the rail. He hadn't skated since the year Y2K was supposed to kill everyone, but he still remembered the mechanics: back foot on the tail, front on the bolts, trust gravity, and pray. Hey, if he was able to max out his skills in lacrosse, football, and tennis in the same school year, surely he could handle this.

He handed the briefcase to Orioles Hat #1, who cradled it like a newborn and immediately tried to open the latch. "It's locked," Lenny said. "Believe me, I've tried."

Purple Hair rolled the loner board over. "Go on, Grandpa. Impress us."

"Oh, Grandpa is it? Hand me the board," Lenny declared with a self-assuredness that caught even him off guard.

He stepped up, feeling the rubbery give under his sneakers. He wobbled, righted, then launched himself at the nearest flat bar. The world narrowed to the sick, exhilarating moment between disaster and physics. He tried to recall every episode of Tony Hawk's Pro Skater, but mostly he just gritted his teeth and hoped to avoid a compound fracture.

First attempt: the board shot out like a bullet, Lenny's legs windmilled, and he landed on his ass. Hard. Second attempt: he made it halfway, the board caught a rock, and he took out a trash can. Third attempt, and he was up, rolling, then—without meaning to—he nailed a grind along the bench, stuck the landing, and then fell clean over the nose into the mulch.

For a second, nobody said anything. Then Purple Hair whooped, pumping her fists. "Yes! That's a new park record for consecutive fails and zero concussions!"

Orioles Hat #1 tossed back the briefcase, grinning. "Alright, old man. You're officially less lame than most mall cops."

Lenny, lying in the mulch, spat out a pine needle and grinned up at them. "Told you I fold better than this crust." He got to his feet, dusted himself off, and did a little bow. "Now, uh, about that drone..."

Purple Hair cocked her head. "Drone?"

He pointed up, and right on cue, the thing hovered into view, blue LEDs blinking a warning. It hovered over the quarter pipe, scanning, then did a slow circle around the park. The kids watched, at first unfazed, then all together too interested.

NASA Hoodie: "That's sick tech. Bet you could buy two of my kidneys with it."

Orioles Hat #2: "You got beef with the government, man?"

Lenny watched the drone, heart thumping. "No, I got beef with a bunch of stalkers that won't leave me alone." He saw their eyes go wide, heard the rustle of curiosity spreading through the group. "You in or not?"

The kids huddled, a brief scrum of profanity and giggles. Then Purple Hair, acting as spokesperson, skated back over. "We got a plan, but you gotta promise us something."

"Anything," Lenny said, maybe too fast.

"Next time you bomb a hill, bring us pizza."

Not even sure what they meant, Lenny shrugged and held up three sticky fingers. "Scout's honor. Now, what's the plan?"

All going beneath a large tree with matching bushes, they broke into rapid-fire strategy. Orioles Hat #1 would skate with the briefcase and Lenny's hat, acting as a decoy. The others would peel off in different directions, criss-crossing the lot to split the drone's attention. Meanwhile, Lenny would lie low by the tree and would make a break for it when the drone got confused.

Simple. Terrifying. Likely to fail.

Perfect.

They split up. Orioles Hat #1 tucked the briefcase under his arm, cranked the board, and launched out of the park at top speed, cutting across the parking lot in a perfect arc. The drone locked onto him instantly, dropping low and pacing his run.

Purple Hair and NASA Hoodie zipped out behind, weaving through the shadows and occasionally flipping off the drone as it hesitated, unsure which kid to follow. Lenny, cramping from his earlier wipeouts, tiptoed across the street, slipping behind a row of orange mesh fencing and hiding behind a pile of cinder blocks. He crouched, counting the seconds.

From here, he watched the show: the kids dodging traffic, popping ollies over parking blocks, the drone whipping back and forth, strobing confusion. It was beautiful, in a dumb, reckless way—like seeing a perfectly timed delivery arrive during a three-alarm kitchen fire.

Eventually, the drone, losing its mind, hovered in place, unsure which target to chase. It bobbed, then zig-zagged, then suddenly shot off after a decoy in a blur of white and blue.

The race started with three cracks of a skateboard on raw concrete, a punchy percussion that echoed off the strip mall facade and up into the shallow, light-polluted sky. Orioles Hat #1, briefcase in tow, jetted down the sidewalk with the grace of a fleeing art thief. The drone, intent on the quarry, kept pace, its whine a constant nagging presence just above streetlamp level.

Lenny was supposed to hold back, hide beneath the tree, but adrenaline made him antsy. He peered through the bushes and watched the decoy crew tear up the block. NASA Hoodie and Purple Hair peeled off in perfect synchrony, splitting the drone's attention and forcing it into a zigzag, every few feet, indecisive about which cluster of moving limbs to pursue.

For a second, Lenny thought it might actually work. Then, almost as if it had a sixth sense for screw-ups, the drone veered off the decoys and doubled back, straight for the tree where he crouched.

He gripped the briefcase tight, and with the raw and unpracticed strength of a man who delivers more pies than he eats, vaulted over the bushes and made a break for it.

The night wind cut against his face, and the briefcase felt twice as heavy, its swinging weight threatening to throw off his center of gravity. He ducked behind an idling food truck, then into the shadow of a nail salon, then up a service ramp that doubled as a skate ramp for the desperate and the damned.

He heard the whoop of a skater, then Purple Hair's voice: "Left, left, LEFT!" He pivoted, saw the crew had looped back and was now leading the drone in a sort of figure-eight through the parking lot, carving tight turns and grinning like escape artists.

Lenny was about to wave a thank you when a hard plastic wheel clipped his heel, and he face-planted onto the curb. For a moment, the world was all taste of blood and the faint aftershock of his own stupidity. Then, hands grabbed him under the armpits and yanked him to his feet.

"C'mon, old dude, keep up!" Orioles Hat #2 said, already pushing him toward the safety of a stairwell.

The drone, for all its smart tech, struggled with the sudden, organic mess of bodies, boards, and erratic movement. For every human decision, it required a calculation, and the kids were nothing if not unpredictable.

They broke through the strip mall gauntlet and spilled onto the open stretch of suburban sidewalk, picking up speed. The drone trailed them, its eye aglow with the blue-white hunger of a digital predator.

Up ahead, NASA Hoodie pointed and called, "The circle! Hit the circle!"

The "circle" was a roundabout, the kind put in to slow down traffic and confuse every driver over the age of sixty. At night, with no cars, it was a launch pad. Orioles Hat #1, clutching the briefcase, hit the curb at an angle, kicked the board up, and landed—miraculously—on the far side, where he spun in a half-circle and flashed a peace sign at the trailing drone.

Lenny was less lucky. He tried to copy the move, got halfway up the curb, then lost momentum and toppled over. He rolled, tucked, and came up wheezing, the briefcase somehow still attached to his hand.

They regrouped behind a bus shelter, catching their breath in the dead zone between the strip mall and the next block. The drone, hesitating, hovered at the intersection, uncertain which pack of skaters to chase.

"Holy shit," Lenny gasped, "this is better than the X-Games." He pressed his back to the plastic wall and tried to will his heartbeat below "exploding piñata" levels.

Purple Hair grinned at him, sweat streaking her forehead. "Dude, you're a maniac. Didn't know you had it in you."

Lenny shrugged, managing a half-smile. "It's the uniform. Brings out the best in me."

Across the street, NASA Hoodie made a break for the drugstore, drawing the drone after him. The others followed, ducking through alleys and weaving between parked cars, always keeping one step ahead of the mechanical tail.

For the first time, Lenny felt not just like prey, but part of a pack.

—

Fourteen miles south, at the edge of a rolling golf course, a mansion lit like a cruise ship at midnight. Inside, the air was climate-controlled, the lighting programmed for maximum "vintage opulence," and a wall-mounted flatscreen split into four camera feeds: drone, street cams, a GPS tracker, and a map of the city pulsing with data points.

Arrayed before the display were the millionaires—Khadijah al-Hari in a sapphire silk robe, legs crossed and radiating catlike calm; Mr. Saito, leaning forward, elbows on knees, gaze fixed and unblinking; Kim So-yeon, tablet in her lap, typing furiously with one hand while the other solved a Rubik's cube; Slick Vic Castellano, not watching but tallying stats and odds on his own notepad; and, slouched deepest into the butter-soft sectional, Olu Goldfinger, sipping a protein smoothie and grinning as the drama unfolded.

On-screen, Lenny's figure flashed in and out of drone focus, alternately clumsy and absurdly lucky, his pizza uniform vivid against the grayscale of midnight Towson.

"Who the hell is this guy?" Khadijah asked, more amused than annoyed. "He's all over the place."

Olu wagged a finger, not taking his eyes off the screen. "Told you, my friend, always wager on the wild card. This is why we play the game."

Saito spoke, soft and precise. "He improvises. It's almost... impressive."

Kim, pausing in her typing, snorted. "Impressive if you're grading on a curve. Statistically, he should have killed himself by now."

Slick Vic finally looked up from his page. "I give him another four hours, max. He's got heart, but he's burning too fast. Odds are converging on a quick collapse." He scribbled a number. "Actually, make that three and change."

Olu raised his smoothie in salute. "Let's make it interesting. Double to charity if he beats the drone. Triple if he does it and still keeps the briefcase."

Khadijah flicked her gold nose ring and considered. "Done. But I want to see what happens if he actually delivers the goods. I like a man who's desperate and just dumb enough to get creative."

Kim shot her a look. "Statistically speaking, desperate people just end up in jail."

"Or in charge," said Saito, with a faint smile. The room hummed with the pleasant static of high-stakes amusement.

They turned back to the screen, where Lenny and his new crew were ramping up the next phase of their escape.

—

They ran it like a playbook. NASA Hoodie, now the primary decoy, broke from the group and made a beeline for the local library, the drone on his tail. Orioles Hat #1 and Purple Hair doubled back to help Lenny, who by now was running on fumes and stubborn optimism.

"We gotta split again," said Orioles. "Otherwise it's just gonna ping-pong between us forever."

"Agreed," Purple Hair added. "But this time, we need a smoke bomb."

Lenny looked around, panicked, then remembered the "extra spicy" red pepper packets he still had in his pocket. "Will this work?" He handed her a wad of the little heat missiles.

She eyed them, then grinned. "We can weaponize it."

They made for the next alley, found a stack of trash bins, and, together, staged a quick-and-dirty bottleneck. Lenny, briefcase in tow, crouched behind a bin, while Purple Hair emptied the pepper packets into a Big Gulp and waited for the drone to round the corner.

It took the bait—zoomed into the alley, lights pulsing, intent on the figure with the case.

Purple Hair popped the lid on the drink and, with the force of a Little League pitcher, lobbed the concoction dead center into the drone's undercarriage.

The world slowed. The drone hesitated, rocked, then did a little wobble as the sticky, nuclear-red slurry hit its rotors. It managed to climb out of reach, but now its camera feed was smeared with synthetic capsicum and high fructose corn syrup. Even at its height, they could hear the engine revving in protest.

Lenny cheered, then instantly regretted it as the drone, in a final act of vengeance, plummeted toward the ground. Like the action star he always wanted to be, Lenny dove out of the way. The world seemed to slow to a crawl as the drone missed them by inches and shattered on the blacktop. It bounced twice, spun, and then lay still, the little red light finally snuffed.

The three of them stared at it, then at each other, then let out the collective, nervous laughter of people who'd nearly died together and couldn't decide if it was the best or worst night of their lives.

"Well," said Lenny, still clutching the briefcase, "that was—"

"Legendary," Purple Hair finished for him.

"You think it was the government?" Orioles Hat #1 nudged the wreckage with his shoe.

"Worse," Lenny said, already scanning the sky for any new threats. "People who only want a piece of my pie," planting his hands firmly on his hips, striking a pose that screamed superhero confidence.

Purple Hair frowned and said, "We should bounce before they send a replacement."

They did, keeping to the shadows, doubling back and cutting through side streets until the suburbia gave way to row houses and midnight silence.

They finally stopped behind a closed bodega, hidden by the shadow of a delivery van. Lenny leaned against the wall, the briefcase against his knee, and tried to remember the last time he felt this alive and this close to cardiac arrest.

"Hey," said Orioles Hat #1, "you sure you're not, like, a spy or something?"

Lenny shook his head. "I wish. I'm just a delivery guy. With bad luck and worse judgment."

Purple Hair cocked an eyebrow. "You gonna tell us what's in the case?"

He looked down at it. For a moment, the world went still— just the cool metal and the pulse in his wrist.

"No idea," he said. "But I'm supposed to deliver it. And after tonight? I'm damn well going to."

They nodded, a silent compact among fugitives and misfits.

—

Back at the mansion, the millionaires watched the final moments of the drone, transfixed.

Olu clapped and slapped his knee. "Unbelievable! He actually did it!"

Saito, eyes narrowed, said, "I underestimated him."

Khadijah smiled, a slow, feline stretch. "I didn't. I want him for the next round."

Kim So-yeon typed, then looked up. "I already have his route mapped to within a hundred yards. Statistically, he'll need to catch a ride. Less surveillance. Higher chance of completion."

Vic shrugged. "Odds are still against him. But I'll admit—he's earned my bet."

The flatscreen replayed the final seconds of the drone's last stand, the blue glow fading to black.

"Double or nothing?" Khadijah asked.

Olu's grin doubled. "You know it, my friend."

They poured themselves another round, eyes fixed on the silent map, betting and watching and wondering what kind of world would let a guy like Lenny Bruno become the last wild card on the board.

—

On the street, Lenny and the kids caught their breath. For the first time all night, the air felt light.

He hoisted the briefcase, set his jaw, and looked up at the sky.

"All right," he said. "I appreciate the help. It was…fun."

"For sure delivery agent," Orioles Hat #1 said.

"You're welcome to the park anytime," Purple Hair said.

Standing tall, "I know I promised pizza the next time I'm around," he said, reaching into his pocket. "Take these," handing them each a coupon for half off an extra-large pizza with two toppings.

With that, he turned and walked away.

And for the first time in a long time, he actually believed he might succeed.

Car Wash Calamity

Lenny Bruno hopped onto a curb, the briefcase tucked tight to his ribs like a fumbled football. The drone was gone—destroyed, but he didn't trust that another one would not appear. Paranoia had its own gravity. It tugged at the base of his skull even as he put blocks between himself and the last debacle.

He surfaced onto the broad edge of York Road, breathless, and took in the late-night carnival of north Baltimore: ambulances slurping up the wounded from the bars, ambulance chasers chasing, cabs and Lyfts stacked in the Chick-fil-A drive-through, and every flavor of undergrad spilling out of patios and onto cracked sidewalks. Neon signs buzzed against the sodium streetlights, and Lenny was so amped on adrenaline that it all looked like a failed Broadway set, held together with old gum and wishful thinking.

He needed transportation. He needed something faster than a hand-me-down skateboard. He needed, and this was not new, a plan. Lenny ducked under a plastic awning and tried to slow his breathing, sweat crawling down the small of his back. He took a frantic inventory: phone, half dead, no ride share apps installed, being that he once had a car of his own; pockets, empty except for two remaining coupons. The briefcase was the only thing worth anything, and it was worth everything, especially now that it felt heavier with each step.

He eyed the curb, scanning for an abandoned bike, a drunk's moped, or just something with more horsepower than what he was riding. The city gave him an answer: a row of electric rental scooters, propped up like toy soldiers at a charging station by the bus stop, each one glistening beneath the streetlights.

He nearly laughed out loud. He figured a higher pepperoni was speaking to him, guiding his path?

He glides over, props up the worn skateboard against the street post, fumbles out his wallet, and tries to read the instructions printed on the handlebars. Too many steps for someone with his resting heart rate, but he got the gist: scan the QR code, swipe the card, ride like hell.

He mashed the code sticker with his phone, the camera shaking as much as his hands. "C'mon, c'mon, c'mon," he muttered, punching in his details. The app demanded his age, blood type, and the answers to three security questions he'd forgotten years ago. He tried "password" and "pizza4life" as many times as it would allow. Finally, it spit out a digital key, and the scooter beeped to life with a smug little chirp.

"Beautiful," Lenny whispered, and straddled the thing, briefcase balanced awkwardly between his knees.

He launched himself forward. The scooter jolted violently, like a wild animal trying to throw him off. Lenny clamped his thighs around the seat, legs trembling as he fought to regain control. The briefcase wobbled precariously, so he wedged it under his armpit, squeezing it tight while flailing his arms like a windmill caught in a storm as he slammed down on the throttle.

In seconds, he was airborne. Not literally, but it felt like it. The wheels spun up, and the battery whine rose above the traffic's drone. He steered with one hand, the other welded to the briefcase. He'd seen YouTube videos of people faceplanting on these things at ten miles an hour, and he was easily clocking twice that, weaving through the crowd of midnight pedestrians like an ambulance that only delivered regret.

The city blurred past: car, people, and the occasional stray animal. He whooshed through a cloud of vape and nearly lost it when a group of lacrosse bros stepped off the curb, forcing him to swerve around a fire hydrant and skid into the crosswalk. Horns blared. Lenny, high on momentum, shot a peace sign and a "Sorry!" over his shoulder, then leaned into the next block.

He squinted at the empty space where a rearview mirror should have been, conjuring images of drone vengeance in his mind. All clear, for now. His delivery uniform whipped around him like a flag caught in a gust, the once-vibrant red now dulled and splattered with urban grime, and an unexpected sprinkle of parmesan that clung on like a stubborn memory of past mishaps.

Lenny squinted at the map in his head. He had to get to Hampden by sunrise, and the clock in the strip mall window said it was already creeping past three. If he didn't make the delivery by then, the bet was off, the quarter-mil vanished, and his one shot at not dying alone in a pizza-stained apartment would shrivel like days-old sausages.

"Must go faster," he muttered as he gripped the handlebars. He knew he was already at top speed, but that did not, for he had to do something to believe it would.

He zipped down the next block, scanning for shortcuts. The north end of town was a maze of alleys, two-way streets pretending to be one-way, and potholes deep enough to store regrets. Lenny hit a speed bump, and for a fleeting heartbeat, he felt the scooter launch him into the air. The world below vanished as he soared, then came crashing down with a jolt that sent sparks flying from the wheels like tiny fireworks.

"Never brake, always swerve," he shouted victoriously, remembering the ancient wisdom of Baltimore's oldest cabbie:

He clung to that advice as he veered through the side streets, dodging recycling bins, a trash fire, and a shirtless guy walking two pit bulls. The city lights got weirder and the buildings closer, the street narrowing to a river of broken glass and regret. He hit a patch of cobblestone, and the world juddered. Every filling in his teeth buzzed. The briefcase, wet from sweaty palms, slipped an inch. He squawked and nearly ate the handlebars, but caught himself at the last second, grinning at his own resilience.

"Nothing keeps a Bruno down!" he shouted to nobody. His voice echoed off the rowhouses, and a car alarm went off two blocks away, as if to cheer him on.

Even as the sidewalk ran out and he had to hop the scooter onto the street proper. Traffic was thinner here, but not friendlier. The one car in sight gunned its engine at the light and rolled coal in Lenny's direction, peppering him with oily mist. He coughed, spat, and used the nearest storm drain as an improvised obstacle, threading the scooter between it and the moving bumper with a millimeter to spare. He cackled, the wild edge of exhaustion making everything funnier.

He took the next alley anyway, hugging the wall and making for the shortcut behind the Planet Fitness. It was here that the briefcase almost betrayed him. The alley was narrow, hemmed in by dumpsters and the wheezing AC units of a closed taco shop. Lenny hunched down, squeezing through a choke point between a Honda Civic and a mossy fence, only for the handlebars to snag on a hanging trash bag.

The bag burst. Out poured a cascade of egg shells, coffee grounds, and what could only be described as "fermented taco surprise." The stink hit him like a slap. Lenny, gagging, let go of the briefcase for half a second to bat the filth away. The case dropped, hanging against the scooter's deck, and nearly tumbled into the wet.

"Nononono—!" Lenny dropped his foot, braked hard, and managed to scoop the briefcase up with one motion, hugging it to his chest as if it were a life preserver and he was lost at sea.

He came to a breathless halt, heart jack-hammering. The city noises faded, replaced by the muted thrum of his own pulse. He stood there, breathing in the heady aroma of old lettuce and victory.

He checked the case for dents. Still locked, still shining, still ticking off the seconds to destiny.

He shivered, both from adrenaline and the thought of what would happen if he failed. The $250,000 danced in his head, each dollar a pixel in the high-def image of a better life.

He gritted his teeth, wiped his hands on his uniform, and remounted. He could see the avenue ahead, the last hurdle before the hill into Hampden. The streets were slick, the sidewalks crowded with the late-night detritus of a city that never really closed.

He roared out of the alley, wove between two parked delivery vans, and aimed for the curb cut. He glanced at the sky, and still there was no drone. But paranoia dies slowly, bringing his eyes back to the road, he was late noticing the sedan backing out of the car wash.

Lenny tried to brake, but his foot slipped. Time dilated as he pulled the handlebars hard to the right.

The sign above read "AquaBlitz: Express Wash" and below it,

in meaner font, "No Entry Once Cycle Begins." The logic was simple: if you went in, you were getting cleaned, ready or not.

Lenny's brain had just enough time to register the warning before the scooter, he, and the briefcase shot into the tunnel at full, unwise speed. The sensor tripped. Sirens whooped. A safety gate slammed down behind him with a pneumatic hiss and the kind of finality usually reserved for prison doors.

For a heartbeat, everything was still. The world, muffled by the car wash's insulation, shrank to the hum of distant machinery and the slick, slow-gliding sound of rubber on wet concrete. Lenny hung there, one foot dragging, hands white-knuckled on the grips, briefcase clenched between his knees. He tried to slow, but the ramp was greased, and gravity did not negotiate.

Ahead, a metal arch bristling with nozzles angled toward him like a SWAT team. Red and green indicator lights blinked in sequence, the traffic signals of doom. Somewhere, a compressor cycled up, and then the jets fired.

The water hit him with the force of a riot cannon. Lenny's face flattened against the scooter stem, eyes popping, beard slicked straight back. His pizza uniform absorbed exactly none of it, and within two seconds, he was soaked through, shoes squishing and collar hanging like a dead fish. The briefcase, momentarily buoyant, tried to wriggle free, but Lenny caught it with a forearm and hugged it close, chest-to-metal, like a drowning man with the world's worst flotation device.

He tried to stand. The jets followed, tracking him with unerring accuracy, pelting him from every angle. The scooter wobbled, the wheels slewing sideways. Lenny steered into the skid, then got punched square in the back by a blast of cold so intense his lungs forgot how to work. He doubled over, then straightened with a yell that only got drowned out by the next barrage.

He squinted ahead, blinking through sheets of water. The tunnel stretched on, a gauntlet of moving parts and corporate sadism. The next obstacle was a set of spinning brushes—giant, sentient loofahs in blue and yellow, churning at chest height.

He thought about stopping, but the car wash had other plans. The scooter's back end got hit with another jet, sending it forward at double speed, and Lenny slammed into the first brush head-on. The bristles slapped him with the wet, soapy strength of a thousand angry car detailers. He spun in place, arms pinwheeling, vision smeared by foam. The briefcase again tried to slip, but Lenny locked his elbow, sandwiching it between his body and the stem.

The brushes alternated directions, and each time he thought he could catch his breath, another set flopped him sideways. His hat flew off, plastered instantly against the wall, and the blue dye leached into his beard in swirling clouds. The only thing holding him upright was the centrifugal force of the brushes and his own freakish will to not be bested by basic machinery.

The pizza uniform, once his only shield, now betrayed him. The polyester turned to cheesecloth, clinging to every inch, funneling the water and suds right to his most sensitive regions. Rainbow soap foamed over him in great heaping dollops, the smell of fake cherries and bad lemon choking the air. For a moment, Lenny considered just letting go, going limp, surrendering to the cleansing power of industry.

But then he remembered: quarter million. Delivery deadline. The world's dumbest gamble. And he remembered Tony's voice in his head—*"Don't ever quit unless you want to end up like dough in the trash."* Lenny gritted his teeth, spat out a glob of blue foam, and rammed the scooter forward, straight into the next phase.

The high-pressure rinse.

This time, the water came warm, then scalding, then cold again. It hammered his eardrums and blinded him for a full five seconds. Lenny screamed, but it came out as a bubbly gurgle. His legs gave up. He rode the scooter like a luge, butt barely hanging on, the briefcase wedged between his knees and threatening to dislocate something important. His feet dragged through the runoff, a Niagara of soapy disaster.

He careened, half-blind, into the wax zone. The nozzles hissed, and the world was sprayed in a fine mist that glued the foam and dirt in place. Lenny's beard, now striped in blue, yellow, and shocking pink, took the brunt of it. He blinked, tried to see through the sticky veneer, and realized his hands were glued to the scooter with some unholy concoction of wax, soap, and the chemical ambition of late-stage capitalism. Or it simply could have been fear taking hold.

The dryer phase announced itself with a roar, the sound of a jet engine at takeoff. Lenny, still clamped to the scooter, was blasted with hot air that inflated his shirt like a life raft and threatened to peel the skin from his cheeks. The briefcase dried instantly. He tumbled forward, feet back on the deck, and braced for whatever final humiliation the car wash could offer. There was, of course, one more set of brushes—now oscillating at max speed, geared to scrape off the last vestiges of dignity.

The scooter shuddered through, Lenny holding on with a prayer and a death grip. The brushes battered him on both sides, thumping the briefcase like it was a pizza dough that owed somebody money. Lenny, battered but undeterred, shot out of the tunnel and onto the exit ramp, trailing rainbow suds and an aftershock of steam.

He coasted to a stop, the scooter's battery finally giving up the ghost. Lenny, dripping, gasping, and caked in a color palette best left to children's birthday cakes, planted both feet on the tarmac and howled in triumph.

He held up the briefcase. Not a scratch.

He held up his other hand. Not a single pizza coupon survived.

His uniform, formerly matted with dirt, was now a tie-dyed disaster, equal parts pride and shame.

He staggered into the open air, shaking himself like a Saint Bernard, and drew in a lungful of crisp, after-midnight breeze. It tasted like gasoline and victory.

"Well, at least I'm clean for my quarter-million payday," he mumbled with a grin, as he wiped his face.

He tucked the briefcase under his arm, shot a salute at the defeated car wash, and limped off into the Baltimore night, ready for whatever the world could throw at him next.

"Deliveries are guaranteed," he said to bolster himself.

Accidental Inspiration

The next delivery was supposed to be simple—point A to B with no side quests, no animals, no stunts, just Lenny, the briefcase, and a city that mostly wanted him to leave it alone. Instead, Lenny had driven all the way downtown and staggered up the slick steps of the Baltimore Convention Center looking like a tie-dyed Jackson Pollock tribute in a cheap polyester uniform, beard full of blue streaks, shoes squelching with every step, and the briefcase welded to his palm as if by trauma or faith. The night air coming from the harbor was brisk, but not nearly enough to dry his uniform or his mood.

Inside, the lobby was a sensory assault of fluorescent lights and carpet patterns designed to obliterate the will to live. The place was jammed, even at three-fifteen in the morning—night owls, insomniac cleaning crews, and the kind of conference weirdos who thought sleep was for the unmotivated. Lenny's eyes adjusted just in time to catch a glimpse of his own reflection in the glass: pizza hat mashed to one side, beard now resembling the afterimage of a snow cone accident, and the uniform—God, the uniform—bleeding a tie-dye Rorschach of shame from shoulder to shoe.

He checked his phone for the twentieth time. The GPS, now operating on 15% battery and pure spite, showed a little blue dot pulsing like a digital aneurysm. "Destination: 415 E Pratt Street," it said, bold as brass. "Estimated time: two minutes ago." Lenny squinted at the lobby signs—banquet hall A, concourse B, some kind of "Mid-Atlantic Youth Entrepreneurship Conference" happening in the upstairs ballrooms—and felt a chill. This wasn't a delivery address. Unless there was a billionaire behind the pizza curtain, he was in the wrong universe.

He thought about cutting his losses and bolting for the nearest exit, but the car wash had done a number on his dignity and balance, and he limped when he ran. He tried anyway, making a beeline for the automatic doors before anyone could stop him.

Too late.

A human hurricane in a headset and orthopedic flats materialized from behind a fake marble column. She clocked him instantly.

"You—are you with the keynote?" Her eyes did a full lap of his outfit, took in the still-dripping beard and psychedelic stains, and—remarkably—did not flinch. In fact, she seemed almost pleased.

"Uh, no?" Lenny said, instinctively hiding the briefcase behind his leg like it was a shoplifted ham.

"Yes. Yes, you are," the woman decided, steamrolling his objections. "You're the resilience guy. You're the only one left. You were supposed to be in green room 2 twenty minutes ago, but I assume you ran into some kind of adventure." Her mouth said "adventure" but her eyes said "meth bender."

Before he could deny it, she hooked an arm through his and towed him off at a dead run, the briefcase thunking against his knee like a stubborn dog.

"Look, lady," Lenny tried, but she shut him down with a

raised finger and a multitasking phone call to the AV crew. "Green Room 2. Now. Keynote is up in eight. No, six. No, he's here now—yes, yes, the pizza stains are intentional, it's his signature. Tell the interns to lay off; this is the brand, apparently. Okay. Thank you." She hung up, shot him a glare that dared him to breathe wrong, and kept moving.

The world blurred past in streaks of vinyl and half-asleep teens wearing name tags. Every turn revealed a new genre of chaos: harried caterers, a sleep-deprived DJ arguing with a podium, a teenager in a cape negotiating with a man in a novelty shark suit. It was like every bad team-building exercise Lenny had ever been forced to endure, multiplied by a hundred and piped directly into his will to live.

He tried to pivot, make a run for the men's room, but the event coordinator was a black belt in crowd control. She bulldozed him through a set of double doors and into a backstage corridor labeled "Authorized Personnel Only." In the sudden hush, she fixed him with a smile that would have made a DMV clerk proud.

"Name?" she demanded, already entering it into a battered clipboard.

"Lenny," he managed. "Lenny Bruno."

She typed it, frowning. "That's not the name on the program."

He panicked. "Stage name. It's, uh, Italian."

She nodded, barely listening, and stabbed a guest badge to his chest. "You're on in five. Makeup will do what they can, but honestly? You look like every other motivational speaker we get after midnight. Just don't throw up on the audience."

She shoved him through another door and vanished. Lenny was alone in Green Room 2, which turned out to be a converted janitor's closet stacked with folding chairs, leftover conference swag, and a table loaded with half-eaten fruit trays. A perky volunteer in a neon t-shirt set him in front of a cracked mirror and dabbed at his beard with a paper towel.

"You're the guy who does all the metaphors, uh, Metaphorman, right?" she asked, not waiting for a response. "Love your stuff. I saw that one video, the 'Sometimes You're the Bird' one. Inspiring."

He stared at her, mute, as she scrubbed at a blue stain on his ear. She powdered it with something that smelled like Play-Doh, then jammed a wireless microphone into his hand.

"Just talk about struggle," she advised. "And adversity. The last guy did, like, a whole ten minutes on how his startup failed and now he's a billionaire, but it bombed. I think the kids want real, you know?"

Lenny glanced at the stack of cue cards beside the fruit. They were covered in bullet points: "OVERCOMING FAILURE," "HUSTLE MINDSET," "UNLEASHING YOUR INNER WARRIOR." He picked one at random. "Rising from the ashes," it said, in Comic Sans.

He could feel the panic rising, a tide of cold sweat and existential dread. He wasn't a motivational speaker. He wasn't even a good liar. All he knew about entrepreneurship was how to get fired with flair, and how to survive on undercooked breadsticks and generic marinara. He was here for a reason.

"You're gonna kill it. Break a leg!" the volunteer said, giving him a double thumbs-up.

She zipped off, leaving him alone with his thoughts, a dying phone, and a stage door that now had two interns stationed outside, presumably to prevent escape.

He tried to text Tony, but the phone died mid-excuse. He considered hiding under the table, but the folding chairs were stacked too high. There was nothing to do but pace, hyperventilate, and practice his opening line.

"What do you say to 200 kids, with one look, will be able to tell I'm a fraud," Lenny thought with each step he took.

Before he could answer that, the door swung open and the event coordinator reappeared, now with a walkie-talkie and a haunted look.

"You're up," she said, and thrust him toward the stage.

Lenny stumbled out, blinking under the assault of stage lights and the expectant silence of 200 faces. The ballroom was a shallow bowl of folding chairs, packed with every flavor of awkward. He could hear a single cough, a stifled snicker, and the click of a thousand phones filming his entrance.

"We present to you Metaphor-man," an announcer's voice boomed over the room's speakers.

He wanted to run, to drop the mic and the briefcase and just go, but the event coordinator's voice was in his ear, half threat and half command: "Just do your thing, then go."

He stepped up to the podium. The briefcase hit the surface with a resonant thud, earning a ripple of laughter from the front row. He tried to smile, but it felt more like a dental emergency. He scanned the room for exits. The only way out was through.

"Uh," he began, voice cracking. "Life is... unpredictable. Sometimes you end up where you don't belong. Sometimes you get chased by goats, or... car washes. But if you hold on tight to what matters—" he thumped the briefcase for effect, "—you'll always have a shot at delivery. No matter what tries to scrub you out."

The teens stared, some bemused, some visibly inspired. Lenny felt a glimmer of hope, or maybe just the onset of a mild stroke.

He leaned into the mic, mustered every ounce of fake confidence, and delivered the only motivational speech he'd ever needed:

"When life knocks you down, get up. Even if you smell like a pizza that's been through a power washer. Especially then. Because that's how you get remembered."

The applause was scattered, but it was applause. Lenny grinned, the world spun, and for a moment, he actually believed he belonged on that stage.

He had no idea what would happen next, but for now, he was delivering. And as always—no extra charge.

For a frozen second, the ballroom was silent except for the soft whir of AV equipment and the distant scream of a Red Bull fridge in the hallway. Lenny gripped the podium, eyes squinting against the lights, and braced for the incoming jeers. He got one weak "WOO!" from the back row and a smattering of polite claps, which was more support than he'd ever gotten at any previous job, parole hearing, or Thanksgiving.

He could have left it there. Could have mumbled an excuse, faked a seizure, and slunk offstage into witness protection. Instead, something clicked inside him—a stubborn, bottom-feeding pride that had never served him well but had always, somehow, kept him going.

He grabbed the microphone, ditching the podium, and paced to the edge of the stage. The crowd of teens—hoodies, and eyeliner—watched, skeptical but expectant. Lenny tapped the mic twice, making sure it was real, then launched into the kind of motivational speech only a human pizza grease fire could deliver.

"Okay," he started. "Life is like a pizza. Sometimes it's hot and ready, sometimes it's cold and disappointing, but you can always reheat your dreams if you just believe in the microwave inside your heart."

The front row burst out laughing. For a second, he thought they were mocking him. Then he saw the kid in the Naruto hoodie wipe a tear from his eye, and he realized: they thought this was intentional.

He doubled down. "Let me tell you, I've delivered more bad pizza than most people eat in a lifetime. I've been lost, I've been undercooked, I've been left out in the rain, and still had to pretend I was fresh-baked. But you know what separates a champion from a crust-crumbler?" He leaned forward, lowering his voice to a conspiratorial stage whisper. "It's the toppings, my friends. It's what you put on top. It's how you dazzle it all up."

Laughter rolled through the crowd like a wave, rising higher with each punchline. In the back, a flickering screen lit up as someone aimed their phone at Lenny, capturing the moment. The tremors in his hands faded away, replaced by a surge of adrenaline. He strode across the stage, brandishing the briefcase above his head as if it were a championship belt won in an epic showdown.

"People ask me all the time—'Lenny, how do you bounce back from failure? How do you keep getting up when the world keeps pushing you down, usually with a coupon for half off next time?' I'll tell you. It's not about the dough. It's about the delivery. Anybody can have a big idea, but can you get it from Point A to Point B without losing your cheese?"

The audience was with him now, not just laughing but actually nodding along, as if they'd just figured out he was performing some kind of Andy Kaufman-style pizza TED talk.

Lenny milked it for all it was worth. "Success is ten percent inspiration and ninety percent perspiration. Just like a good pizza is ten percent sauce and ninety percent not screwing up the delivery." He let that sink in, then paced a slow circle. "Have you ever opened a box and found everything slid to one side? That's not destiny, that's physics, and sometimes physics is a jerk. But you get another chance. You can pick it up, put it back together, and try again by pushing all the cheese and toppings where they belong. Sometimes you gotta eat your mistakes. That's how you get stronger."

A kid in the third row raised a hand, earnest as a Sunday school volunteer. "What if you get fired from every job, like, ever?"

Lenny grinned. "Join the club. You're looking at the un-defeated regional champ getting canned. You know what I learned? If you can't be the best at something, be the best at bouncing back. Nobody remembers the perfect pizza, but everybody remembers the one that caught on fire and still showed up on time."

Someone in the crowd started a slow clap. Others joined. Lenny's confidence ballooned to dangerous proportions.

He leaned into the last part, lowering his voice like a real speaker. "Every day is a new pizza. You can change the toppings, the crust, the whole style if you want. But the secret ingredient is you. You're the one who makes it unique. Don't let anybody tell you you're too cheesy, or too weird, or too outside the delivery zone. If you want it, go for it. Just make sure you tip yourself at the end."

That actually got applause. Real, unfiltered, honest applause from a roomful of strangers. Lenny soaked it in, felt the blue streaks in his beard dry under the heat of their approval, and—for the first time in forever—felt like maybe he had something worth saying.

He gave the crowd a two-fingered salute and tossed the mic in the air, nearly dropping it but catching it with a showman's flair.

"Alright, that's my time. Remember, life's a pizza. Don't let it get cold," he said with the most genuine smile.

The teens howled. Even the jaded AV techs in the wings smiled. Lenny bowed, briefcase aloft, and basked in the euphoria of a thousand Instagram stories hitting the cloud all at once before turning to exit backstage.

He had no idea what he'd just said, but it didn't matter. For five glorious minutes, he was more than a delivery guy. He was the goddamn pie in the sky.

He was, finally, the main course.

The instant Lenny stepped off the stage, it was like dropping a fresh slice into a tank of starving turtles. The audience didn't just clap; they surged forward, a foaming tide of teenage energy, phones held high and voices echoing his speech back at him in a chorus of meme-ready soundbites.

"You're the crust, man! You're the crust!" someone shouted from the second row.

"I'm gonna reheat my dreams!" another yelled, fist-pumping so hard he lost a vape pen in the process.

Lenny stumbled backstage, dazed, as a wall of humanity pressed in for selfies. The briefcase nearly dislocated his elbow with every flash, but he clung to it, a beacon in a sea of chaotic affirmation. He tried to retreat to the green room, but three kids with lanyards blocked the door, peppering him with questions about "personal branding" and "going viral." One asked if he had an agent. One asked if he was single. One just asked for a pizza.

He gave them all the same answer: "Never deliver cold,

always deliver bold." It was nonsense, but they ate it up.

At the edge of the room, the event coordinator stood frozen, headset askew, frantically poking at her iPad with the increasing desperation of a passenger searching for the emergency brake on a runaway train.

"Who booked him?" she hissed into the radio. "You're telling me this is not Metaphor-man. Then who is he? I want him on the schedule. There's no one in the green room. He's not in the database. I need to know who this man is!"

But the kids didn't care. They wanted their slice of the pie, even if it came with a side of weird.

Lenny, now the center of an impromptu meet-and-greet, fielded questions about everything from social anxiety to startup failure to his beard maintenance routine. He made up answers as he went. "Moisturize with olive oil, and if your dreams dry out, just dip 'em in ranch." They lapped it up, every word.

Somewhere near the back of the crowd, a group of AV techs replayed the stream on their phones, already cutting it into TikTok-sized segments. One of them nodded in approval. "Dude's got content," he said, "and a look. The stains are next-level."

Meanwhile, in her car, its windows lit with the blue-white pulse of her phone. Khadijah al-Hari reclined on the leather seating, phone in hand, appraising the viral sensation with a clinical detachment that would have chilled most mortals.

At first, out of boredom, she'd gazed out the window as the world passed by. The city seemed to have gone stale, and nothing delighted her more than thinking she had gained the upper hand on her competitors.

But then the feed from the "YouthCon" went wild, first with

whispers of an unscheduled pizza guy, then with the full-on eruption of memes and madness.

She watched as Lenny, soaking wet and tie-dyed, spun pizza metaphors into gold, holding the crowd in the palm of his sudsy hand. She paused the video on his face—a strange mask of bravado, panic, and something else. Something she recognized.

Ambition.

She smiled, slow and deliberate, and flicked the video forward, scanning for weaknesses, tells, anything she could use. There was nothing obvious. He was too raw, too unfiltered. She liked that.

With one hand, she opened a text thread—marked only with an emoji of a single black domino—and typed: "Find out who this pizza deliverer really is."

The reply came back instantly. "Already on it."

She set the phone aside, eyes narrowed in delight, and let the city's current of chaos run its course.

Back at the convention center, the party was reaching a fever pitch. Lenny had been hoisted onto someone's shoulders, the briefcase raised like a trophy, and the crowd chanted his name. "LEN-NY! LEN-NY!" Even the event coordinator had given up trying to restore order, retreating to the far side of the stage with a look that said she was updating her resume in real time.

Lenny tried to make a graceful exit, but the teens followed him down the hall, cameras rolling. He offered them advice on everything—relationships ("Don't let your pizza get cold, if you know what I mean"), business ("Sometimes you're the box, sometimes you're the pizza, but never the napkin"), and even life's big questions ("If you hit rock bottom, bounce. It's what rocks do.").

Eventually, security arrived—not to escort him out, but to

clear a path through the mob of new fans. Lenny surfed the wave to the main entrance, breathless and still not quite believing what had happened.

He looked down at the briefcase, now more battered than before, but still locked and waiting for its true delivery.

For a second, he wondered if he could just stay here, live off the energy of being an accidental legend. But as the crowd thinned and the cold air hit him, he remembered the mission, the money, and the weird sense of destiny that had gotten him this far.

He squared his shoulders, zipped up the ruined uniform, and headed for the door, already composing his next motivational speech in his head.

Because sometimes, the best you can do is keep moving forward, even if the only thing waiting for you is the next disaster.

And if it involved pizza, all the better.

"If you hit rock bottom, bounce. It's what rocks do," he mused with a smile.

The Algorithm Apocalypse

If you hit rock bottom, bounce. It's what rocks do, he'd said.

Lenny Bruno believed it, or at least had spent the last forty minutes bluffing hard enough to fool every last YouthCon kid, the event coordinator, and even the cleaning crew who watched him empty the hospitality fruit tray like a man on a farewell tour. The applause from the ballroom still tickled his ears, along with the endless notifications from a suddenly active phone battery resurrected by the sheer will of WiFi, or possibly the attention of several million new fans.

Now, at a little past four, Lenny jogged the cracked sidewalks of downtown Baltimore, heading for the destination that had haunted his night: the casino where Mr. Saito held dominion over chance itself. Each footfall squished, his uniform a tie-dye shroud still damp from the industrial rinse and peppered with stains that looked even more radioactive under the orange streetlights. His beard, once a proud salt-and-pepper mane, now veined with streaks of blue and red, gave him the aspect of an aging punk rocker who'd lost a bet with a rainbow.

Across the street, the casino glowed with the hunger of a billion LEDs. Its facade was a carnival of moving lights, all beckoning, promising, threatening. A massive screen on the corner displayed a repeating video of a woman with diamond teeth grinning as she stacked poker chips, and Lenny, breathless, had a weird moment of recognition before he realized it was one of Saito's regulars, probably Ms. Khadijah al-Hari herself. She flicked her hand on the video, and the screen shimmered into a graphic of champagne bottles tumbling in zero gravity.

Lenny checked his watch. He was early. In fact, he was hours ahead of the deadline, which was either a miracle or a mistake. He'd lost all track of the other millionaires' bets, the progress of the rival delivery crews, or whether Tony would ever forgive him for ditching the party order. But right now, the world had funneled down to a single moment: Lenny Bruno, armed with the briefcase, standing on the wet asphalt of destiny.

He cradled the case with both hands, holding it not as a courier but as a victor clutching the grail at the end of a mythic relay. It was heavier than he remembered, either from the added weight of expectation or because his arms had simply given up for the night. He'd survived a berserk goat, a personal drone vendetta, a car wash engineered by Bond villains, and a full-body public humiliation at the hands of 200 hypercritical teens.

"Let's see them automate that," he whispered, grinning at his own reflection in the darkened window of a vape shop.

The shop's security glass distorted his features, giving him a funhouse jaw and carnival eyes, but the briefcase was crystal clear—a silver bullet, streaked with city grime and battle scars.

He paused on the curb, eyeing the casino's main doors. No valets, no security, just a lazy drift of gamblers and insomniacs, all looking to lose something before morning. He debated walking in—just striding up to the front desk and demanding an audience with Mr. Saito—but the energy wasn't right. Lenny wanted a second to savor the finish line. He wanted to walk a victory lap around the block, maybe rehearse a few quips for when he handed over the case.

He detoured through the parking lot, dodging the puddles, and found a lonely patch of curb behind a dumpster. From here, the casino was just a wall of pulsing light, and Lenny felt invisible enough to take a breather. He dropped the briefcase between his sneakers and pulled out his phone, scrolling through the tidal wave of notifications.

Most of it was nonsense—memes, mentions, video snippets of his viral speech edited to include a thousand animated pizzas—but buried in the chatter was an update from the delivery app. It pinged: "Final Destination: Confirmed."

Lenny smiled and pumped a fist.

"Take that, Saito," he muttered, then immediately worried that the casino was bugged and that Saito himself was listening in.

He checked over his shoulder, but only a rat the size of a dachshund regarded him from under the dumpster.

He knelt to adjust the latches on the case, fingers skidding on the wet metal. That's when he noticed the lock—specifically, the part of the lock that now bulged outward from the surface, as if something had tried to claw its way free. The casing was warped, and a faint, sour aroma wafted from the seam, one part battery acid and two parts "not my problem."

Lenny squinted. The digital readout on the lock was fritzing, numbers blinking in a random pulse, the kind of behavior that made him think of the time he'd microwaved an old cell phone for "science." He tapped the display. Nothing. He rapped the side of the case with his knuckle, and the display flashed briefly, then died.

It occurred to him, with the slow bloom of existential terror, that if the lock failed completely, the entire delivery could be null and void. Did the millionaires specify it had to be "unopened"? What if the case was now a live bomb or, worse, a failed crypto wallet?

He wet his lips, glancing around as if the shadows might spill secrets. A mental scale tipped in his mind, balancing the thrill of discovery against the potential fallout, reminiscent of a half-hearted student cramming for a pop quiz. With a quick breath and a flicker of mischief in his eyes, he made up his mind: this was the perfect moment to sneak a look, when the world was blissfully unaware and the chance to feign innocence still lingered like an unspent dollar bill.

He hoisted the case, glancing left and right. The parking lot was deserted except for a couple making out under a streetlamp and the rat, now gnawing on something unidentifiable. Lenny ducked behind a low wall, shielded from both the casino and the street, and set the briefcase on his lap. He tried the latch. It resisted at first, the water-damaged lock sticky and swollen, but with a little leverage from a keychain bottle opener, the mechanism gave a weak "click." The screen flickered. The lock cycled through one last, desperate sequence of numbers, then went dark.

Lenny exhaled, the cloud of his breath mingling with the faint chemical vapor from the briefcase. His hands trembled, a residual charge of nerves and anticipation, as he pressed his thumb to the release. He hesitated for a second—just long enough to consider what Tony would say, what Saito would do, what the universe expected from a man with nothing left to lose.

He pressed down.

The lid parted with a hiss, like a soda can on a summer day. For a split second, Lenny imagined a swirl of white smoke, a

Genie or a ghost or a pizza-loving wraith, but there was only the metallic tang of electronics and the faintest hum from inside the case.

He sat there, the case cracked but not yet open, every muscle in his body ready to run or scream or both.

But in the end, curiosity was a stronger force than fear. Lenny Bruno, haunted by every bad decision in his life but still unwilling to quit, pried the briefcase the rest of the way open and peered inside.

Whatever was in there, he'd be the first to know.

And, just maybe, the last.

He had expected something heavier, like a brick of diamonds or a bag of unmarked bills, but what greeted Lenny inside the briefcase was a pair of objects cradled in bespoke foam: a hard drive, glossy and logo-free, and a small, square television no bigger than a takeout box, its screen black but humming with a low, expectant current. The interior was both precise and overkill, the foam cut to exact tolerances, not a millimeter of waste.

He poked at the drive, lifted it out, then gently replaced it. The screen glared up at him, its reflection catching the sickly yellow parking lot lights. Lenny shivered; for a moment, he imagined the thing was watching him.

Then the TV powered on.

He hadn't touched anything, but the moment his shadow crossed the lens, the screen shimmered, filled with static, and resolved into a video feed. Not just any video. The opening shot was a slow pan over the Baltimore skyline, every landmark aglow and slightly sharper than reality. At the bottom of the screen, a ticker scrolled:

THE FUTURE OF DELIVERY, TODAY.

Lenny's jaw worked soundlessly. He eyed the hard drive, then back at the screen, then the drive again. In his head, a slot machine spun with possible explanations—none of which made sense, and all of which spelled disaster.

The video cut to a man in a charcoal suit, perfectly still at a brushed-steel podium. Even in 480p, Mr. Saito's presence was palpable. His hair was so black it bordered on unnatural, his jaw a geometry problem, his smile as thin as fishing line.

"Welcome, esteemed colleagues and partners," the video Saito intoned, in a voice so even it might have been AI. "And congratulations on being selected for the pilot of our new solution."

Lenny's fingers twitched. The parking lot seemed suddenly colder.

In the video, Saito swept a hand across a 3D city map. "We all know the problems with traditional delivery. Human error. Theft. Inefficiency. Cost. What if you could eliminate them, at once?"

The ticker changed: INNOVATION DOESN'T WAIT FOR REG-ULATION.

"We bring you the Pizza Delivery Optimization Algorithm," Saito announced, his smile widening to reveal the infamous diamond grillz. For a split second, Lenny thought he saw his own reflection, minuscule and wild-eyed, in the glinting stones.

The video split-screened: On the left, a sweating man in a delivery uniform (not unlike Lenny himself, though more kempt) fumbled three boxes while tripping over a dog leash. On the right, a sleek, unmarked vehicle zipped to a stop, and a small drone emerged, clutching a pizza with a precision that was both surgical and disturbing.

"In field tests, our AI beat the fastest human drivers by

a median margin of 33.7%. That's nearly one-third more deliveries, on time, every time. Zero errors. Zero complaints."

Another cut: graphs, bar charts, a scrolling list of driver names—all flagged "OBSOLETE" in red as the AI line surged upward.

"We know what you're thinking," Saito said, his tone shifting to a friendly neighbor selling insurance. "What about the human touch? The smile? The local knowledge?" He leaned in. "We've studied that, too."

The screen now showed an algorithmically generated Lenny, complete with stubbled chin and a hat at the same wrong angle. It greeted a simulated customer, recited a joke, and finished with a signature phrase: "Delivery guaranteed."

Lenny felt the color drain from his face. He watched his own digital ghost do a double fist-bump and laugh a little too hard at its own joke.

The real Saito reappeared. "By automating empathy and improvisation, we have not only matched the human element but improved upon it. Our customer satisfaction ratings have risen to 4.97 out of 5."

The ticker: CUTTING HUMAN COST, INCREASING CUS-TOMER VALUE.

The video was now a barrage of stats, time-lapses of human drivers dwindling as the AI ramped up, a projection that within six months, "legacy staff" would be completely phased out.

Lenny's hand, still clutching the foam lining, went numb. The numbers blurred. The video was a trap, and he'd walked right into it. He was delivering the very thing that would put him—and every other night-stalker, wage-slave, and screw-up—out of business for good.

He tried to breathe, but his lungs disagreed.

The video Saito finished with a flourish. "This system is designed to be deployed by the best. If you are watching this, you have already been selected. Welcome to the next level."

The screen went black, save for a single line of text:

DELIVER TO SAITO'S CASINO. DESTROY AFTER VIEWING.

Lenny stared. He ran a hand through his ruined beard and stared some more. It took a solid minute before he could form words, and when he did, they came out in a whisper.

"Holy mother of all calzones," he breathed.

The hard drive and TV sat mute, their job complete. Lenny looked around, like someone might leap out and tell him this was a prank, a set-up, a weird lesson in supply chain efficiency.

But the only thing that looked back was the rat, which, at this point, seemed to be his last coworker.

He sat there in the cold, clutching the briefcase and the scraps of his future, and wondered if it was too late to reroute the delivery to the bottom of the Inner Harbor.

For a few seconds, Lenny just sat on the ground, leaning against the wall, letting the cold seep through the polyester and into his bones. He'd spent all night outrunning failure, skipping over disaster like stones on a pond, but now it finally caught up to him, squatting on his chest with all the grace of a wet anchovy.

He tried, at first, to process it quietly. Maybe if he ignored the reality, it would evaporate, like bad cheese left in the sun. But the words on the black screen burned brighter the longer he stared:

DELIVER TO SAITO'S CASINO. DESTROY AFTER VIEWING.

His brain started to sizzle.

"Holy... pepperoni," he breathed, then louder, "Holy PEP-PERONI!" He snapped the briefcase shut and started pacing the alley like a zoo animal denied its hourly enrichment. "What in the deep-dish hell is this? You dirty, double-sauced bastards!"

He aimed the rant at the darkness, but the only audience was the rat, now perched on the lip of the dumpster, whiskers twitching with interest.

"You—" Lenny jabbed a finger at the case, "—are a sacrilegious sausage scheme, that's what you are! A mechanized betrayal! A garlic knot with a microchip!"

He flung out his arms, gesturing wildly. The briefcase flew open again, and the dead screen flashed for a split second, as if mocking him. Lenny turned a circle, clutching at his beard, then reeled off another round:

"They want to automate me? The nerve! I got more guts in my left pizza pocket than all the CPUs in this city!" He stomped the ground, sending a thin spray of standing water up his pants. "Replace me with a robot! Why not just program the customers to tip better, you soulless—"

He didn't finish the sentence because he spotted movement out of the corner of his eye. A shadow detached from the mouth of the alley, sidled closer, and then resolved into a skinny teenager in a conference lanyard, phone held out in front of him like a crucifix.

The kid's thumb waggled on the screen, and for a second, Lenny thought he was dialing 911. Then he saw the red streaming dot and realized, with horror, that the meltdown had an audience. A big one.

"Yo, check it out! He's losing his mind!" the teen said into the mic, grinning like a raccoon with a stolen wallet. "Dude's screaming about pizza robots. Actual meltdown, right here, live!"

He pivoted the phone, and the chat exploded across the

bottom:

PIZZA GUY RAGE!!!

Is this real?

Bro needs extra cheese LMAO

#HumanSauce

Lenny blinked at the camera, stunned. Then the true weight of humiliation landed on him like a second, hotter anchovy.

He tried to cover his face, but the kid only zoomed in, narrating: "He's clutching the case like it's a puppy! Oh my god, he's… is he crying? Are those real tears?"

"They're not tears!" Lenny bellowed. "It's rain, or allergies, or—"

But the chat was already off and running:

Crying over pizza—mood

Will the robot hug him?

Robots don't cry

#TeamDrone

The crowd in the stream doubled in seconds, then doubled again. Lenny, panic rising, lurched toward the teen.

"Give me that!" he barked, hand out. The teen just danced backwards, never missing a frame.

"You're famous, man! This is legendary content! From hero to zero," the teen mocked.

"It's not content, it's—" Lenny stopped.

He realized that now, not only was he jobless, but he was also the world's biggest meme. He pictured Saito and the others, back at the mansion, laughing their grillz off.

He glanced at the rat, now vanished into the trash, the only soul with enough sense to run from this mess.

Lenny slumped, then tried one last time to salvage dignity. He squared up, looked straight into the camera, and delivered in his best customer service voice:

"You want automation? You want efficiency? Fine! But nobody—NOBODY—delivers like Lenny Bruno!" He raised the briefcase in a two-handed salute. "Even if you replace me, I'll always be a step ahead! You can't code hunger, you can't program heart! So stick that in your algorithm and—"

He paused, thinking of a way to finish, then just yelled, "DELIVER IT!" at the top of his lungs.

The stream chat, now a waterfall, went nuts:

KING SHIT

I want him to deliver my pizza

#PizzaRevolt

#TeamLenny

The kid stopped, finally, stunned by the performance.

Lenny, breathing heavily, wiped the sweat off his brow, then nodded to the camera. "That's all for now. Tip your drivers. Goodnight."

He turned and stormed off, the briefcase under his arm, dignity ragged but somehow more intact than before.

The stream cut out, but the legend was just beginning.

The Rise of the Pizza Baron

It was always colder at the mansion after a losing hand. Even in the bloom of summer, the air held a flat, refrigerated charge, like the world's most expensive meat locker, designed to keep the flavor of old money from spoiling. The night's poker marathon had left the airless rooms of the estate with an aftertaste of spent Scotch and the sharper, private scents of self-loathing and victory.

They filed out in order of finish, as was tradition. First, Olu and Khadijah—gliding down the marble stairs with the exaggerated, syncopated grace of con artists who'd already called to their chauffeur. Next, Slick Vic, whose shirt collar could have served as a dueling weapon. He gave the grand foyer one last audit, as if he expected to catch a misplaced decimal point hiding in the wainscoting.

Kim So-yeon came last, trailing the group with her trademark blankness, which made her impossible to read and even less possible to forget. She paused at the landing, watched the others disappear, and only then clicked the Rubik's cube in her hand back into her pocket.

Saito stood alone in the long shadow of the balcony, not so much overlooked as deliberately ignored. He liked it that way. It was in these negative spaces that he did his best work.

Below, the circular drive was full of hush: no birds, no wind, just the ambient whirr of distant pool pumps and the soft, buffered engine notes of the waiting luxury sedans. The drivers, trained to invisibility, remained motionless behind tinted glass. Only when one of the millionaires made a move did a car door open—always with a gentle thunk, never a slam.

The glass doors at the bottom of the staircase slid open with the hydraulic sigh of money. Saito took the steps with the same patience he brought to every hand of cards, not a single one wasted. If he could have minimized the carbon footprint of each step, he would have, and maybe had.

The others lingered at the edge of the drive, performing a last round of ritualized small talk, the kind only people who have never worried about car payments can perfect. Olu boomed a laugh so hearty it could have powered the hot tub, while Khadijah's gold nose ring caught the porch lights and made it look like she was perpetually about to sneeze diamonds. Slick Vic murmured something about "the spread" and "liquidity," and no one laughed, not even So-yeon, who didn't so much as blink.

Saito waited at the threshold, letting the interplay settle before stepping into the fray. The group rearranged itself instinctively, giving him a berth like an unseen forcefield had just powered on. The twins stopped mid-conversation, Vic's phone vanished back into his jacket, and So-yeon, if anything, looked slightly less alive.

Nobody said his name, but every glance was a silent invocation.

He approached his vehicle—an obsidian-black Maybach, glass so deep and dark it appeared to consume the light around it—and waited. The driver, perfectly nondescript, emerged with the punctuality of a metronome and held the rear door, gaze fixed at the shoe level.

The others watched with the detached curiosity of people who have seen every plot twist twice. Saito, without ever directly looking at them, offered a shallow bow. This was not gratitude. It was an acknowledgement: You are here, I am here, we both know what matters.

Olu, emboldened by the vodka, grinned and shouted, "Good game, Saito! Until next time!" His voice echoed off the porte-cochère, flattening the moment.

Saito smiled, the diamond grillz lighting up beneath his lip like a band of coded LEDs. He gave a small, precise nod, then slid into the Maybach, body folding into the custom leather as if it were a home he'd never left.

The interior was cooled to exactly 61 degrees. The driver, who went by "Eli" on the rare occasion he was spoken to, closed the door with the delicacy of a pianist.

The mansion's lights slowly disappeared as they pulled away. Saito reclined, watching the navigation map trace their route in silent, incremental blips. He rested his hand on the armrest, fingers moving in a precise, repetitive tap: a staccato Morse code, spelling out secrets in a language only he knew.

As the driveway receded, the chorus of the mansion faded to nothing. Saito was left alone with the low hum of the road and his own, perfectly measured thoughts.

The Maybach tracked the curves of Charles Street with algo-rithmic smoothness, each turn anticipated and sanded down to a velvet edge by German engineering. Saito's reflection wavered in the tinted window, a ghost overlaying the city, following him as the car slipped past row homes and shuttered carryouts.

He watched the world in passing: drenched with light like a

tattoo parlor, a trio of giggling college girls balanced on cheap stilettos, the sullen sentinels of a closed hardware store. Saito cataloged them automatically, labeling each with a half-spoken heuristic. Risk factor, future value, anomaly quotient. It was how he kept his mind limber between moves.

As they merged with the arterial sprawl of North Avenue, Saito's gaze snagged on a familiar artifact: a battered, yellow delivery car, hatchback sagging under the weight of a pizza sign bolted to its roof. The vehicle's alignment was an insult to physics, its brakes a polite suggestion. Yet it soldiered on, barreling through yellow lights with the suicidal optimism only minimum-wage desperation could engineer.

The sight, at once so ordinary and so specifically targeted at his brain's pleasure center, triggered a memory.

Not a recent one—nothing from the years of engineered adulthood, nothing from the mansions or the night schools of Wall Street. This was old code, written in a language he'd tried to overwrite but never quite deleted.

—

The house had smelled of warm plastic and leftover rice. The living room doubled as a shrine to 80s electronics—his father's CRT, his mother's "miracle" treadmill, the mesh tower fan whirring in the corner, even on days when the heat was off. Saito, age nine, inhabited a corner of the kitchen table, tethered to his father's castoff PC by a tangle of scrounged power cords. His hands hovered over the keyboard, fingers quivering in anticipation, the rest of his body locked in the kind of absolute stillness that made even the clock hands sound rude.

It was late, always late, when he did his best work. His

parents' voices came through the cracked bedroom door, alternating between affectionate Korean and the kind of exhausted sighs that suggested the future was already behind them. Sometimes he could hear the neighbor kid—a full year older and a full head taller—playing kickball in the street, the slaps and shouts echoing up through the floorboards like a war zone he'd never be drafted into.

Saito ignored it all. His universe fit in thirteen diagonal inches and one blue-tinted CRT. He was rewriting the pathfinding logic on a shareware version of Lode Runner, trying to shave the average time-to-goal by a full second. It was the kind of math that made him dizzy, the best kind, and when the code finally compiled, he pressed ENTER and—

There was a knock.

He froze. Not his parents; they had perfected the art of silent movement, a trait he sometimes suspected was hereditary. The knock again, now with the urgency of a customer demanding service, and a third, softer rap that sounded less like a demand and more like a secret handshake.

His mother, always the first responder, shuffled to the door. A cold gust filled the house, bringing with it a sharp tang of garlic, burnt cheese, and the chemical sweetness of tomato paste. Saito's stomach, heretofore content to run on fumes, lurched.

"Delivery," called a voice, pitched to slice through parental anxiety.

He left the computer, a crime punishable by death in his own mind, and tiptoed to the threshold. There, bathed in the raw sodium of the porch light, stood the pizza guy: a minor deity in the pantheon of his childhood, cap turned backwards, hands stained a permanent orange from pizza grease. The man held out a box as if offering a lost relic.

Saito's mother, mortified by the unexpected opulence, tried to hide her slippers with one foot. "No tip, sorry," she whispered, like she'd lost a bet.

The pizza guy just grinned, nodding like he'd seen it all before, and passed the box across the threshold.

Saito took it from his mother's hands, feeling the heat radiate through the thin cardboard. There was a magic in that first breath—the convergence of yeast and acid, the ghost of something savory hovering above the cheap black-and-white logo. The box was heavier than he'd expected, the weight promising a meal that would both feed and exceed.

He carried it to the kitchen table, clearing a landing zone by a stack of books. The box hissed open. Steam poured out, rippling over the keys. The pie was perfect: a disk of pure intention, golden with a lacquer of melted cheese, crust only slightly charred, cut into mathematically precise wedges. No slice was bigger than any other. Even the bubbles in the cheese arranged themselves into a Fibonacci sequence.

He pinched a slice at the tip and lifted it, strings of cheese stretching to breaking, then curling back in on themselves like the springs inside a clock. The first bite burned his mouth. He loved it. The pain was a confirmation of the real, the now. The crust gave just enough; the sauce was, by some miracle, neither too sweet nor too sour. There was a hint of basil, a whisper of crushed red pepper, and—most wondrous of all—a single olive, embedded like a dark planet at the edge of a slice. He ate that piece first, then another, then another, until his fingers shone and bore the evidence of his feast.

He remembered nothing of the code he wrote that night, only the taste, the speed, and the certainty that this—this—was what it meant to win.

—

Saito blinked, the ghost of cheese and basil faded as he returned back to reality, while the Maybach drifted to a stop at a red light. The driver, Eli, glanced in the rearview, searching for cues, but Saito gave him none. He preferred the silence, the way it allowed the past to run its simulations unimpeded. He flexed his fingers and smiled a tiny, private smile.

Everything about the city was designed to distract, to reroute, to tempt the brain off course. But Saito, now as then, was immune. He had tasted perfection, and he would not be denied it again. He closed his eyes and let the car carry him the rest of the way home.

The Maybach came to a halt. Moments later, Eli had opened the door, and Saito eloquently exited. Immediately, he the vibrant neon glow of Saito's magnum opus, the Saucy Casino envelops him like a warm embrace. The Saucy Casino, a place where dreams are made, where money is made, and where pizza is made.

The entrance is a riot of colors, with oversized pizza slices and playful pepperoni graphics adorning the walls, making it feel less like a gambling den and more like a whimsical carnival for adults. A giant spinning pizza wheel greets newcomers, its bright red and green sections promising everything from free garlic knots to high-stakes poker games.

Inside, the air is thick with the mouthwatering aroma of fresh-baked dough mingling with the clinking sounds of chips and laughter. The casino floor sprawls out before him, an eclectic mix of gaming tables shaped like oversized pizzas—

tomato-red roulette wheels spin alongside mozzarella stick poker tables where players huddle over their cards, eyes glinting with anticipation.

The lighting is dim but punctuated by twinkling fairy lights strung across the ceiling like stars in a culinary galaxy. Wait-staff weave through the crowd, balancing trays piled high with slices that steam in the cool air—each bite promising to be as thrilling as any gamble on the floor.

Saito strides forward, his presence commanding attention amidst this playful chaos; even here, he exudes quiet authority. Patrons glance up from their games as he passes, some offering nods of respect while others can't help but chuckle at the absurdity surrounding them—the man who turned pizza into an empire now walks among them like a king surveying his kingdom made entirely of cheese and chance. He never thought that his empire would all come from one delivery of pizza as a kid.

"The house always wins," he mused, a triumphant grin curling at the edge of his lips.

Dough or Die

The Baltimore city bus rolled through the empty dark like a psychiatric ward on wheels, all white linoleum and sickly fluorescent light, every surface just a little too shiny for comfort. At the back, stretched out across three seats like a man who'd been exiled from the kingdom of normal people, Lenny Bruno rode alone, the briefcase heavy on his lap and heavier in his mind. Each lurch of the bus over a pothole sent a jolt up his tailbone and threatened to shake loose the fragments of what was left of his dignity.

He felt watched, even though the only other living souls on the vehicle were the driver, a guy in a reflective vest who looked like he'd been in a union since infancy, and, halfway up the aisle, a slumped figure in a hoodie, dead asleep or pretending to be. Lenny would have put money on "pretending," because no one in Baltimore slept that hard, not even the people in comas.

The briefcase sat upright on his knees, closed and locked and streaked with the fingerprints of his entire evening. He caught his own gaze and held it, as if staring down a rival he'd met in a previous life. The Lenny in the metal was a mess: blue streaks still lining his beard, collar warped from a car wash, sauce stains forming a constellation across his chest. There was something about the eyes, though—wide and wild, but still holding a glint of hope, the last speck of optimism clinging to the ship as it slid beneath the waves.

He let out a long, bone-deep sigh that fogged the case and turned his reflection into a spectral blur.

"So," he said to the briefcase, or maybe to the other Lenny inside it, "this is the part where you ask yourself: Was it worth it?"

The case didn't answer, but the sleeping guy three rows up twitched.

Lenny shifted, peeling his thighs from the vinyl seat. He weighed the case in his hands, feeling the cold promise of all the jobs it would kill, all the lives it would upend, all the dreams it would automate. He pictured Saito's face, the diamond grillz flashing as he declared the "future of pizza," and he wondered if the man had ever even eaten a pizza delivered by a real, flesh-and-blood human.

He tilted the case toward the window, watching as the passing streetlights carved lines across his double. For a moment, he saw himself as the world saw him: a punchline in a borrowed uniform, caught between the end of one era and the start of something worse. He tried to muster outrage, but all that came up was a tired, aching hunger—for carbs, for meaning, for the chance to go back to a time when the worst thing a pizza delivery guy had to worry about was a tip stiff or a rabid dog.

The bus shuddered to a stop at a red light. The driver glanced up at the rearview, caught Lenny's eye, and gave him the look reserved for the city's most lost souls. Lenny nodded back because at this hour, solidarity was about all he had left.

He wiped the fog from the case and tried again. This time, he spoke to the reflection as if it were a business partner.

"Look," he said, "it's two hundred and fifty grand. Quarter-mil. You do the job, you buy a new car, pay off the debt, maybe even open your own shop. Get Tony off your back. You do it, you win. If you don't do it…" He shrugged. "You're just a punchline with a hero complex and a negative checking account."

His reflection seemed unimpressed.

Lenny scowled, the weariness in his shoulders turning into something sharper. He jabbed a finger at the case. "But if you do it—if you just hand this thing over, no questions, no fight, no nothing—you're the reason they put you out of a job in the first place. You're proving them right. You're disposable. Replaceable. Not even worth a coupon, let alone a pension."

The words echoed in the empty bus, bouncing off the hard plastic and coming back with twice the force.

The hoodie guy grunted, shifted position, and began to snore in earnest, the kind of snore that sounded like a wet vacuum cleaning up after a frat party.

Lenny braced his elbows on his knees, leaned in close, and stared into the eyes of his enemy.

"Alright, Lenny," he said softly, "what's it gonna be? Sell your soul and take the money, or torch the whole damn thing and maybe go down as the patron saint of obsolete humans?"

The bus jerked back into motion, the engine wheezing like an asthmatic walrus, and the question hung in the air, unanswered.

For a long minute, he just rode the bumps, letting the drone of the road lull him into a trance. He let his mind wander to the faces of the skate kids back in Towson, the band of misfits who'd risked road rash and injury to help a stranger with a briefcase. He thought about Tony, and the way the old man could turn a ten-word insult into a motivational seminar, and how he'd probably just laugh if he ever saw the inside of that case.

He thought about the kids at the YouthCon, the way they'd chanted his name, the brief moment when he was more than just a delivery guy, more than just the butt of a joke. For a second, he let himself believe he could be something else—something better.

Then the bus hit a pothole the size of Lake Superior, and the case jumped into his arms. The impact snapped him out of his reverie, and he gripped the handle tight, afraid for a second that it would burst open and spray the contents all over the aisle.

He imagined the scene: circuit boards and AI modules spilling everywhere, the driver slamming on the brakes, the hoodie guy snapping to attention and yelling "Terminator!" at the top of his lungs.

Lenny snorted, a real laugh, and the sound startled even himself. He looked down at his reflection and, for the first time all night, gave it a conspiratorial wink.

"Just you and me, buddy," he whispered. "Maybe, we'll just figure this out."

The bus rolled on, carving its way through the sleeping city. Lenny's eyelids drooped. The case grew heavier, the seat warmer, the world softer at the edges. In the faint hum of the wheels, he heard the voice of every pizza he'd ever delivered, every shortcut he'd ever mapped, every dumb joke he'd ever made to a customer who just wanted him gone.

He looked at the case one last time and saw not a mirror, but a window. Beyond it, the world he'd spent his life navigating— messy, irrational, filled with people who would always choose weird over perfect.

He shut his eyes, and for a few precious minutes, let the city carry him home.

With Rock Bottom Comes Reheated Ambitions

The first step into Tony Martinelli's Pizzeria brought with it the screech of a rubber sole, the reek of chlorine mop water, and the accusatory stare of the Virgin Mary from her perch atop the napkin dispenser. For Lenny Bruno, the effect was both homecoming and execution. Every scuffed inch of the floor was a court record; every chip in the Formica booth a prior conviction.

He shuffled past the soda fountain. It was well into the morning, but Tony Martinelli's was never really empty, as it was one of the late-night pizza places open. The only other patrons were a pair of security guards working through a double shift and a family-sized pepperoni, and a tired delivery girl tallying receipts at the far end of the counter. Behind the glass, Tony himself presided, sleeves rolled high, veins like steel cables writhing beneath his flour-dusted forearms. He was assembling the next day's dough, but the moment Lenny crossed the threshold, Tony's eyes locked on, like a scope.

"Bruno," Tony said, voice flat as day-old focaccia. "You either got mugged by Jackson Pollock or you finally made manager at Domino's."

Lenny felt the words hit, solid and immediate. He did not

flinch. He did not reply. But only shuffled onward.

Tony set down the mixing bowl and emerged from behind the counter, wiping his hands on the world's least sanitary rag. "Where's the car, Lenny?" he said, the way some men ask about a missing child. "You lose the keys, or did you trade it for a new sense of shame?"

Lenny paused, looked up. The glare from the kitchen made halos around Tony's head. "Car's fine," he lied. "It's on a lone dark road, like my life."

Tony snorted. "No car, no deliveries. You really want to tell what's going on?"

He didn't wait for an answer. He stomped to the front, flipped the "Open" sign to "Closed," and nodded at the counter girl to finish up. The security guards had already lost interest; one was dozing, the other was mining his phone for lottery numbers.

Lenny let the silence thicken. He dropped the briefcase on the nearest table and collapsed into a booth, the vinyl sighing beneath his weight. He reached for the nearest pizza box, popped the lid, and stared into a cold, congealed landscape of sausage, peppers, and the blank, unsalted stares of banana peppers.

Tony came over, arms folded. He regarded Lenny for a long, narrow moment. "You gonna tell me where you been?"

Lenny did not meet his eyes. He peeled a slice from the pie and let it droop, the cheese gone stiff, the crust already drying at the edge. He took a savage bite and chewed without tasting.

"Out," he said, mouth half full. "And all around town."

Tony's lips twitched. "You trying out for drama club now?"

Lenny ignored him. He worked his way through the slice, then the next, all the while staring into the unmoving pizza as if it were an oracle or a confession booth. The urge to talk built inside him, hot and shameful. It was a familiar compulsion, one he usually fought with sarcasm or deflection, but tonight he was too tired to run.

"I was sliced and diced by fate, Tony," he began, dropping his voice into a gravelly near-whisper. "Chased down alleys, beaten by cheese, left out too long like yesterday's deep dish."

Tony rolled his eyes, but stayed. "Let me get this straight. You ghost me for half a shift, come back looking like a Jackson Pollock victim, and want me to feel bad for you because you had a little existential crisis on the job?"

Lenny put down the third slice. He pressed both palms to his face, then ran his fingers through his beard. "If only it were so simple, boss. But life isn't a twelve-inch with easy cuts. It's a never-ending special, and every time you think you're done, the kitchen just keeps sending out more."

Tony shook his head. "This is the worst monologue I've heard since I got cable. What happened to the simple Bruno, the one who only whined about tips and a broken GPS?"

Lenny grinned, the expression more a baring of teeth than a smile. "He died. Out on a delivery. May he rest in thin-crust peace."

He stared at the pizza, then back at Tony. "You ever feel like the universe is just waiting for you to mess up, and every time you dodge disaster, it just gets more creative?"

"Every day since I hired you," Tony deadpanned.

Lenny barked a laugh, sharp and real. For a second, the mask slipped, and the raw, pulpy mess beneath showed through. He felt it. He wanted to spill it all out—the drone, the goat, the briefcase, the AI. But he didn't. Not yet.

He picked at a crust, stripping it down to its naked, floury backbone. "You know what the worst part is, Tony? I didn't even screw up. I did everything right. I hustled. I delivered. I kept the dream alive. And what do I get?" He held up the pizza crust, waggling it like a bony finger. "Obsolescence. Irrelevance. Outpaced by a hunk of silicon and a bad internet connection."

Tony regarded him in silence, then leaned in, arms on the table. "Listen, Lenny. Maybe you ain't cut out for the classics. Maybe you're more of a frozen aisle kinda guy. But you show up, you do the job, and as long as you don't burn the place down, you get paid. It's not complicated," he smiled.

Lenny let the words sink in. He wanted to believe them. He wanted to be the kind of guy who just let things happen, who didn't fight every shift of fortune like a cornered rat. But he couldn't. Not anymore.

He looked down at his hands, knuckles scraped from the city. He felt the weight of the briefcase at his feet. "Ever think about what you'd do if you weren't the king of cheese?" he asked quietly.

Tony didn't answer. He just stared, the expression on his face sliding from mockery to something softer, sadder, almost... parental.

The closing staff made a show of ignoring the scene, but Lenny could feel their eyes on him, the way they always watched for cracks in the armor.

He took another slice, this time tearing it in half before eating it, the gesture violent, almost petulant.

"I guess I thought if I just kept moving, kept improvising, the universe would get tired and let me win one," Lenny said, voice muffled by food. "But I'm not sure it works that way."

Tony picked up the rag and wiped down the table, the motion slow and deliberate. "Sometimes the dough rises, sometimes it falls. Sometimes you get lucky, sometimes you get..." He gestured at Lenny's uniform, "Whatever happened to that?"

"Yeah," Lenny finished for him. "Sometimes you get what you deserve."

They sat in silence, the only sound the hum of the refrigeration and the soft, distant snoring of the security guard.

Lenny finished the slice. He wiped his hands on a napkin, then balled it up and stared at it.

He didn't cry. Not really. But for a second, his eyes burned, and he blamed it on the banana peppers.

Tony watched, arms crossed, face a question mark.

Tony didn't waste another beat. He flipped a damp rag directly onto Lenny's face.

Lenny peeled it off slowly. "You always throw like that, or just at the walking dead?"

"Only at the ones who can't get up on their own," Tony said, voice even but with a hard edge under it.

Before either of them could get another word out, the front door banged open, hitting the wall with a sound like a gunshot.

Into the pizzeria strode a man who had clearly never heard of personal boundaries or subtlety. Uncle Red—Baltimore's premier conspiracy theorist, part-time street oracle, and Lenny's blood relative in the most regrettable sense—with his collar popped, and pants two inches too short. Though it was night, his face was shrouded by an oversized pair of aviators and, for reasons unknown, continued to sport his fake mustache pasted right over his real, better mustache.

He paused in the doorway, looking at the closed sign as though wondering how he got in. After a moment, he inhaled deeply and bellowed, "The eagle lands at Tony's! Repeat: the EAGLE lands AT TONY'S!"

Every head in the pizzeria snapped up—even the ones that

weren't attached to bodies.

Uncle Red made a beeline for Lenny's booth, trailing the scent of department-store cologne and the more subtle note of recent confinement. "Gentlemen," he said, sliding into the booth next to Lenny without invitation. "Are we clear to speak openly? Or is the ravioli bugged?" He tapped the pizza box with a finger, nodding to himself as if it had confirmed a password.

Tony glared. "If you're here to sell black-market cable again, I'll call the cops. Matter of fact, I'll just have security throw you out."

Red waved him off, already reaching for a slice. "The pizza is not the message, my good man. The pizza is the medium." He bit off half a slice in one go, talking as he chewed. "But that's not why I'm here. I'm here for my nephew. The Package Handler. The Man With the Plan."

Lenny shrank into his seat. "Can you keep it down, Uncle Red? Some people are trying to have a nervous breakdown."

Red slapped Lenny on the back, nearly dislocating a vertebra. "No time for breakdowns, Leonard! The signal has been intercepted. The briefcase is the key, and the city is the lock. You, my friend, are the only one left who can pick it."

Tony raised an eyebrow. "What's he talking about, Lenny?"

Lenny shook his head. "He's talking about his own brain. It's like three goats in a trench coat fighting over the steering wheel."

Uncle Red ignored the barb, leaning close enough that Lenny could count the nose hairs through his sunglasses. "Listen up. The Goat bleats at midnight only when the pizza's cold, but the drone flies at dawn when the truth must be told."

Tony looked at Lenny, deadpan. "Is this contagious?"

Lenny shrugged. "Doctors say it skips a generation. Lucky

you."

Red snatched another slice and began to draw diagrams in the grease on the table. "The world is an oven, Lenny. And right now, the wrong hands are reaching for the knob. You got two options: get baked, or be the baker."

Lenny blinked. "That's not how ovens work."

Red jabbed the air with the slice. "You're not hearing me, kid. This is a global play. The guy in the casino? He's the cheese. He's melting all over the city. But he's got holes, see? You gotta be the mouse."

Tony watched the spectacle with a mixture of horror and intrigue. "You believe any of this, Bruno?"

Lenny hesitated. He looked at Red, at the wild, unfiltered panic in his eyes, and realized—for the first time all night—he didn't feel quite so alone.

"I think," Lenny said, slowly, "that the universe is out to get me. But maybe... maybe it needs my help."

Tony snorted. "You're both nuts. But you're my kind of nuts."

The kitchen door swung open. The closing staff, sensing a disturbance in the Force, peered out, wide-eyed. One of them whispered, "Is that the Baltimore oracle?" The other just nodded and started recording on her phone.

Red reached for the briefcase, but Lenny beat him to it. He gripped it tight, a lifeline, a bomb, a punchline all at once.

He looked at Tony. "You ever see a future where a guy like me can matter?"

Tony shrugged. "Only if you stop screwing around and start acting like it."

Uncle Red was halfway through an allegory about the Mafia, the IRS, and a suitcase full of "exploding anchovies" when Lenny felt something click. Not in his brain—his brain had stopped tracking about three metaphors ago—but somewhere deeper, a spot he'd reserved for gut instincts, irrational plans, and the memory of every time he'd beaten the house odds by sheer dumb luck.

Red rapped the table, pizza grease pooling around his knuckles, and intoned, "It's like I always said, Leonard—if you want to expose the sauce, you gotta peel back the cheese. Only then will the true pepperoni surface."

Lenny stared at his uncle. The words shimmered, scrambled, then settled like sediment at the bottom of a glass. He felt the shift—not gradual, not gentle, but like waking up on a trampoline: one second flat, the next second airborne.

He sat up straight, hands slamming the table. "That's it," he said, the realization hitting so hard it nearly gave him a nosebleed. "We don't just deliver the briefcase. We deliver the story. We deliver the truth, hot and fresh and straight to Saito's face."

Tony glanced up from his calculator app, which he'd been using as a shield against the madness. "You're having a stroke, aren't you?"

"No, Tony. I'm having a revolution." Lenny was on his feet now, pacing the tiles with the unsteady grace of a man whose body had forgotten sleep and blood sugar in equal measure. "We walk into the casino. We make the handoff. But not before we blow the lid off their whole scam. We go public. We live-stream the exchange. We turn their own evil scheme into a viral marketing disaster."

Uncle Red beamed, pride leaking from every pore. "See, Tony? I told you he was the smart one. Not like my sister's kids, who still think Little Caesars is a real Italian."

Tony looked up at the ceiling, as if expecting divine intervention, then back at Lenny. "And you think Saito's just gonna let you walk in, wave a phone, and embarrass him? That's not how billionaires operate. That's how you get vanished and buried under the freezer."

Lenny kept pacing, words coming faster now, his arms windmilling like an air traffic controller on too much espresso. "That's the beauty of it, Tony. We're not heroes, we're bait. He expects us to screw up. He's counting on it. We make the delivery, just like he wants. Only this time, the pizza guy gets the last word."

A staffer, mop in hand, had stopped pretending to clean and was openly gawking at the commotion. Another poked her head around the kitchen door, snapping photos like she was at the zoo and the animals were doing a trick.

Uncle Red, never one to let a captive audience escape, stood up on the bench and cupped his hands around his mouth. "People of the Pizzeria! This is not a drill! Tonight, we stand on the edge of a global reset. The time has come to reclaim our birthright as deliverers of destiny!" He pointed at Lenny, nearly toppling over in excitement. "This man is the crust. We are the toppings. Together, we will feed the world!"

Lenny had to admit, it did sound a little better with the crowd involved.

Tony shook his head, but his face had softened, the gruffness bled away by something like hope—or at least the desire to see how the chaos played out. "You're serious about this," he said, not as a question, but as a reluctant confession.

"As a heart attack," Lenny replied. "Which, considering this diet, is pretty damn serious."

Tony closed his eyes, took a slow, deliberate breath, then opened them. "Fine. We do this. But if anyone asks, you stole the uniform."

The kitchen staff, which included Scylla and a pair of pink-haired twins, emboldened, abandoned their posts and clustered around the table, forming an impromptu war council. There was no hierarchy, no plan, just a rising chorus of "What if we...?" and "Could we maybe...?" and "Is it legal to bring pizza into a casino?"

Lenny pulled the briefcase up onto the table, thumping it like a judge with a gavel. "First, we need a way to get inside. Saito's got goons at every door. They know me and would try to take the package, and if they see Red, they'll call animal control."

Red grinned, flashing a mouthful of ill-fitting dentures. "Disguises. I got a trunk full of 'em. Fake mustaches, wigs, two priest outfits, and one nun. We can blend in, confuse the cameras."

Tony frowned. "You know that makes us look more suspicious, right?"

A kid from the back piped up, "My cousin works security at the Saucy Casino. He says nobody checks the catering trucks. We just load you in with the food delivery."

A moment of silence, then all eyes turned to Tony.

He shrugged. "You ever see me in a hairnet, Bruno?"

Red whooped, pumping his fist. "Operation Double-Stuffed is a go!"

Tony rolled his eyes, but there was pride in it. "Just promise me you'll keep your pants on outside."

"Only if the mission demands it!" Red crowed, nearly taking out a stack of parmesan shakers in his enthusiasm.

Lenny looked around the room. These weren't superheroes. They weren't even regular heroes. They were the kind of people who lived shift to shift, who knew disappointment as a first language, who never got the best slices. But tonight, in the fluorescent glow of Tony's, they looked like the world's last, best hope.

He stood up on the booth, raised the battered briefcase high, and declared, "We deliver. No matter what. We deliver on time."

The staff roared, a rolling, ragged cheer that shook the windows and scared away the last remnants of self-doubt.

Tony, wiping his hands on his apron, strode to the front and completely locked the door, then turned to his troops. "Alright, Bruno. You got one night. What's the plan?"

Lenny grinned, feeling the old adrenaline spike in his veins. "We bake the biggest pie Baltimore's ever seen. And when it hits, everyone gets a slice."

They huddled around the table, mapping routes and making calls, the smell of hope and pepperoni thick in the air.

Before the sun rises, the world would change.

If this was the last supper, at least it came with extra cheese.

Pie Hard with a Vengeance

For a brief, sacred moment before dawn, the only thing standing between Lenny Bruno and destiny was a parking lot now glazed in rain and a hundred yards of open concrete leading up to Mr. Saito's casino, the city's football stadium loomed in the background. At the edge of the lot, beneath the wan glow of a busted sodium lamp, the team assembled in final formation: Lenny, Tony, Uncle Red, and the four least jail-averse pizza workers.

They were all in costume. That was the first, and most immediate, problem.

Uncle Red had brought the disguises, and Uncle Red did not do subtle. Their "chef" uniforms were less Super Mario, more Spirit Halloween meets Italian funeral. Every hat was a foot tall, white as a dental waiting room, and rimmed in red velvet piping. The mustaches looked like they'd been harvested from a herd of feral possums. Each apron was embroidered "CHEF SUPREMO" in sequins and then smeared with enough stage-blood pizza sauce to trigger a crime scene investigation.

Tony wore his with a grim, resigned dignity, as if he'd once studied under Gordon Ramsay and this was the final punishment for dropping out. Lenny, for his part, leaned into the bit; he'd twisted his fake mustache into a Salvador Dali snarl, and wore his hat at such an angle that it actively disrupted his depth perception. The pizza workers—the two wiry twins, and Scylla, who Lenny believed to have been fired twice already—looked like the world's most flavorless flash mob.

Uncle Red had, for some reason, dressed as a French chef. "International flair," he'd said, twirling his own mustache (over his real one, still visible beneath the glue). He'd also stuffed two entire baguettes up each sleeve, which made his arms comically rigid and constantly in danger of knocking over anything within a five-foot radius.

Together, they surveyed the casino: a three-story rectangle with a false front shaped like a giant pizza box, the word SAUCY spelled out in LED strips. Pepperoni coins, rendered ten feet across, rotated slowly atop the roof, throwing blood-red light across the sidewalk. A security fence pulsed along the back perimeter, lit up in alternating bands of cheese yellow and jalapeno green.

The sky was the color of raw dough, sickly and not quite ready. Somewhere in the distance, a gull screamed.

"Alright, crew," Tony grunted, scanning the lot for cameras and lowlife. "Remember, straight to the loading dock. In, out, nobody gets smart. If you see security, don't run—walk like you belong."

Lenny checked the briefcase, then checked his own reflection in the side window of a parked Civic. He looked like the bastard child of an Olive Garden and a witness protection program.

"Ready," he said, trying to sound like he wasn't already planning his first parole hearing.

Uncle Red waggled his fake mustache at Lenny. "Remember, the code word is 'breadsticks.' If it goes sideways, we split up and meet at the Chuck E. Cheese on Fleet Street."

Lenny snorted. "That's still open?"

"Not legally," Red replied. "But that's what makes it good cover."

Shaking his head, Tony was already on the move, shuffling low along the fence. Scylla and the twins followed, practicing in the art of walking like you hadn't done anything wrong—yet. Lenny brought up the rear, the briefcase wedged under his arm and his chef's hat threatening to take flight at every gust of wind.

They reached the rear fence. The pulsing LEDs were more for show than substance, but the actual barrier was double-wired and topped with razor ribbon. On the other side, the employee entrance glowed like a promise and a threat.

Uncle Red, the self-styled "tech guy" of the operation, had brought a crowbar and a can of spray cheese. The plan was simple: brute force, then sabotage. It became immediately less simple when Red swung the crowbar, and the fence did not so much as dent.

"Sturdier than advertised," Tony muttered.

Red sprayed the cheese at the join, muttering something about "corrosion." The cheese dripped down, coating the wires in a slick, orange mess.

Lenny watched the spectacle, then reached into his own pocket, extracting a travel-sized bottle of pizza sauce. He held it up, the label still smeared with Tony Martinelli's house logo.

"I saw this on a movie once," Lenny said, unscrewing the cap.

Tony side-eyed him. "You get all your science from movies?"

"I get all my science from desperation, boss." He squeezed the bottle, drizzling a thick red line across the keypad and into the casing that controlled the rear gate. The sauce oozed into the panel's seams, dripping down onto the exposed wiring below.

Nothing happened.

Then, with a sound like a microwave full of cutlery, the panel sparked, smoked, and coughed out a blue-white sizzle. All along the fence, the LEDs flickered, then died. The security line shut off with the audible relief of a city block losing power after a heat wave.

Lenny's co-workers cheered quietly. Even Tony looked impressed.

"Nice work, MacGyver," he said.

Lenny grinned, teeth framed by the worst mustache in North America. "Science," he said, just to savor the word.

They scaled the fence and dropped into the wet lot and sprinted across. At the building, they hustled low along the wall, ducking beneath the kitchen's exhaust fans.

Halfway along the building, Uncle Red tripped on a novelty trash can shaped. He landed in a puddle and let out a yelp that was instantly, universally shushed.

Tony glared. "You wanna get us made, Red? How you gonna hide from the FBI when you don't know how to even sneak?

"I'm telling you it came out of nowhere," Red said with a loud whisper, as he popped up and wiped drips of water from his mustache.

"Well, maybe do a cartwheel next time," Tony said.

"Hey, don't give me that, I was just...testing the perimeter, that's all. Oh, and it's clear by the way," Red finished and slid back into position.

They pressed on, reaching the loading dock. Here, the casino's true colors showed: the doors were painted to resemble open mouths, with glowing "fire" decals licking the edges. A sign over the threshold read: EMPLOYEES AND HIGH ROLLERS

ONLY. Next to it, a smaller sign: DELIVERY DRIVERS, USE SIDE ENTRANCE.

Lenny rolled his eyes. "Figures."

They crept toward the side entrance, and just as Lenny's coworker had predicted, the door swung open with a soft creak, revealing an empty corridor. Heartbeats echoed in their ears as they slipped inside, darting through back hallways that smelled faintly of garlic and grease. They passed by the kitchen, where the rhythmic thud of dough being pounded mingled with the sizzle of pans.

As they entered a sprawling hall, the twins and Scylla helped to form a protective barrier around the briefcase, eyes darting for any sign of interruption. Tony stepped forward, adjusting his disguise with purpose, his broad shoulders squared like a soldier ready for battle.

Finally, after what felt like an eternity, they pushed up a set of swinging doors and entered The Saucy. The casino was a fever dream. The floor was checkerboard linoleum, every tile the color of a different pizza topping. The air shimmered with a haze of oregano and neon. Every table was circular, topped with a lazy Susan and a stack of menus, even though nobody seemed to be ordering food.

At the far end, the central pit loomed: a giant, sunken area where dealers in matching chef hats flung chips and cards with practiced bravado. Above the pit, a chandelier made of interlocking pizza peels glowed like the world's classiest Italian wedding. On the stage to the left, a magician in a pizza-box tuxedo sawed a woman in half with a pizza wheel.

Uncle Red's jaw dropped. "It's like Willy Wonka got a yeast infection."

Tony elbowed him. "Focus. Find Saito."

Lenny scanned the crowd, trying to spot their mark. He saw nothing but a rolling tide of night owls, big spenders, and professional weirdos.

"Let's move," Lenny said. "Heads down, straight shot."

They set off, weaving through the chaos. Every few steps, someone called out "Hey, Chef!" or tried to bum a breadstick. Uncle Red played the role perfectly, bowing and offering imaginary baguettes. The pizza workers ducked and darted, never letting the briefcase out of sight.

Halfway to the pit, they hit their first real obstacle: a security guard, arms crossed, blocking the route to the VIP section.

The guard looked them up and down, then grunted. "You guys are late. Saito's expecting the delivery. You know the way?"

Tony nodded, cool as a frozen meatball. "Of course. First time at the new joint."

The guard thumbed a button, opening the velvet rope. "Don't mess up the carpet. Boss gets mad."

They hustled through, Lenny's heart thumping double-time.

Down a hallway lined with pizza murals and framed black-and-white photos of Saito shaking hands with various low-level politicians, two in particular being the mayor and governor, they reached the final door: embossed in gold, etched with a cartoon of a man tossing pizza dough into the stratosphere.

Lenny paused, checked the briefcase one more time, and tried to remember why he'd ever wanted anything more than this: a job, a crew, a shot at doing something dumb and beautiful.

He squared his hat, sucked in a lungful of pepperoni-scented air, and knocked.

This was it. The crust, the core, the center of the pie. No turning back.

He looked at Tony. "Ready?"

Tony nodded, solemn as a funeral.

Uncle Red shot a thumbs-up, glancing back at the others who responded with enthusiastic nods of agreement.

The door swung open. The future, and all its nightmares, waited on the other side.

The casino's inner sanctum was nothing like the rest. Here, the air was colder, the lights sharper, and every table was shaped like a disc of obsidian pizza stone, laser-cut and polished to the point that Lenny could see his own distorted reflection staring back at him with cartoonish anxiety. The décor was a pizza fever dream: slot machines spat out tokens shaped like pepperoni slices, the cocktail napkins were printed to resemble grease-stained pizza boxes, and the servers glided by in tuxedos with dough-colored cumberbunds.

Lenny took it in with a slow, giddy dread. Uncle Red muttered something about "Deep State parmesan" and flexed his baguette arms, but even his confidence had waned. Scylla and the twins hung back, heads down, while Tony marched forward like he'd rather take a bullet than a loss.

At the very center, under a spotlight so bright it buzzed, waited the millionaires. They were arrayed with the formal gravity of a firing squad, each flanked by their own retinue of pale assistants and tech interns. At the head, Mr. Saito sat in a throne carved to resemble a mound of stacked pizza boxes. The grillz on his teeth flashed with each syllable as he spoke low and conspiratorial to his neighbors.

To his right: Khadijah al-Hari, in a tailored sheath dress that shimmered between shades of mozzarella and burnt crust, nose ring polished, lips pursed in an expression that screamed "I want to see you beg."

Next to her was Olu Goldfinger, the one who incited the delivery in the first place. He wore a caftan the color of pizza sauce and drummed his fingers on a gold-plated protein shaker with visible impatience. Beside Olu, Kim So-yeon hunched over a tablet, her bob so sharp it could cut salami, eyes flicking between three different data feeds as she tried to multitask her way to a higher plane of existence.

Last was Slick Vic Castellano, jacket off, sleeves rolled, hands flying over an ancient mechanical calculator as if he could will the odds in his favor by raw kinetic energy.

At a signal from Saito, a pair of security guards in mozzarella-white blazers stepped aside, and the war council of Tony's Pizzeria was ushered forward.

Lenny felt his knees go slushy. He almost tripped over his own chef's clogs, but caught himself at the last moment, setting the briefcase on the table with a clack that reverberated through the room.

Saito raised a finger. "Let the record show," he intoned, "that the delivery deadline was sunrise. You are," he checked his diamond-encrusted watch, "four minutes late."

A ripple of derision passed down the millionaire bench. Khadijah arched a single eyebrow, her gold nose ring glinting with predatory amusement. Olu let out a deep, theatrical sigh and shook his head, lips twisted into a martyred smile.

Lenny felt his face flush, but Tony grabbed his shoulder and squeezed. "You want to nitpick delivery time?" Tony said, voice thick with scorn. "We bled for this order. There's sauce on the streets, Saito."

Slick Vic never looked up from his calculator. "All that matters is the time stamp," he said, voice clipped, "and your guy missed the window. Odds are odds."

Saito steepled his fingers. "Gentlemen, and ladies. The game is the game. If you can't deliver, you can't win. It's nothing personal, just the algorithm." He nodded to Kim, who clicked over to a digital time log, the numbers flickering in her reflection.

For a half-second, Lenny almost let it go. Almost let himself believe that the universe would never, ever let him win one. But then he remembered the YouthCon kids, the pizza workers, Tony, even the goddamn goat.

He squared his shoulders, licked his lips, and said, "That's where you're wrong."

The millionaires leaned in as one.

Lenny fished his phone from his pocket, hands trembling only slightly. He held it up so the clock display faced the group.

"Sunrise isn't until six-oh-eight," Lenny said, "and by my count, it's six-oh-seven, and thirty-eight seconds." He looked straight at Kim So-yeon. "Check it. The weather app is never wrong. And if you think it is, call the National Observatory."

For a moment, there was only the hum of the air conditioner and the clacking of Slick Vic's calculator.

Kim So-yeon looked up, unblinking. "He's correct. Civil sunrise is in twenty-two seconds."

Saito's lips pulled back in something halfway between a smile and a snarl.

Lenny took a breath, savoring it, and then—on impulse— waited. He let the silence stretch, let Saito's eye twitch, let every muscle in the room pull taut.

Then the first rays of actual sunlight blazed through the casino's east-facing window, shooting across the floor and hitting the briefcase dead center. The metal case glowed, lit up by nature and destiny.

Lenny planted both hands on the briefcase, raising it high, "Delivery guaranteed!" He shouted triumphantly.

Uncle Red, unable to help himself, let out a low whistle. Tony looked like he might start weeping, or commit arson, or both.

For one perfect instant, the world held its breath.

Then Saito clapped once. The sound was harsh, surgical.

"Impressive, Mr. Bruno. Very impressive." He pushed back from the table and stood, jacket falling open to reveal a silk tie embroidered with rows of tiny pizza cutters. "You met the letter of the law, if not the spirit."

Olu, never missing a beat, leaned in and grinned. "My friend, you are the wildest wild card. I salute you."

Khadijah, with a smile as sharp as her cheekbones, said, "I prefer my surprises cold, but I admit—this is... delicious."

Slick Vic finally looked up, gave a micro-nod of respect, then went back to tallying ruin.

Saito eyed the case, then Lenny. "I suppose you want your reward?"

Lenny felt the urge to giggle. He tamped it down. "It's all about the delivery."

Saito motioned to a waiting intern, who produced a thick envelope and slid it across the table.

Lenny stared at it, not daring to touch it. He checked the faces of his team—the pizza workers, even Uncle Red, standing straight and proud as the moment dawned.

But Saito wasn't done.

He leaned over the table, hands pressed flat, voice so soft it felt like a trap. "Do you know what's in the briefcase, Mr. Bruno?"

Lenny shrugged. "Does it matter? You wanted it here, I brought it."

Saito's smile widened. "That's the thing. Sometimes, the package isn't just for the receiver. Sometimes, it's for the messenger."

He flipped a switch under the table. All at once, every screen in the casino lit up, even the slots and the ordering kiosks. The image on each was the same: a looping video of Lenny's own viral meltdown from the alleyway, replayed in glorious, HD agony. The meme that had started as a joke was now the wallpaper of every device in the building.

The room erupted in laughter, a thousand voices braying, jeering, and celebrating.

For a second, Lenny felt the old, familiar humiliation rise. He wanted to crawl under the table, bury himself in the garbage bin, walk out, and never be seen again.

But then he looked at Tony, at Uncle Red, at Scylla and the twins who risked joining for a bit of excitement.

Then it hit him like a ton of dough, *"As long as the briefcase remains closed,"* Lenny repeated Saito's words in his head from the mansion. Through all the drama that had occurred over the night, it had slipped his mind.

Had he risked everything and lost.

For a full thirty seconds after victory, it felt as though the entire room was holding its breath. He should have known that some millionaires were simply just allowing him to walk out with the money and call it a night.

"Lenny, you opened the briefcase. Therefore, the deal is off. Regardless if you delivered on time," Saito said with a smirk at the corner of his lips. "My plans are well baked."

Lenny took in the faces of the crowd—the millionaires, their underlings, the casino's staff, even a handful of gamblers still clutching their pepperoni slot tokens in disbelief. And in those faces, he read the same question on them. *What's going to happen next?*

"*It's not going to go down like this,*" Lenny muttered to himself.

He hopped up on the pizza-stone table, nearly slipping on the polished surface, and raised both arms high. The crowd stilled, as if the entire building had sucked in a single, greasy breath.

"Listen up!" Lenny shouted, letting the sauce-scarred chef's hat amplify his voice. "You don't know me. But if you do, I'm not here for your money—" he paused, "Well, maybe a little for the money. But mostly, I'm here for every person who ever showed up late for a shift and still made it work! I'm here for the underdogs, the doughboys, the night crawlers who bleed for your tips and still get replaced by a hunk of code!"

Someone—maybe Uncle Red, maybe not—let out a rebel yell. Tony grunted approval. Even Saito looked impressed, for about half a second.

"The tyranny of Saito's AI pizza system, held in this briefcase, must not come to pass!" Lenny declared, voice rising to a dramatic pitch he'd only ever used in high school drama club. "We're not just delivery people, we're dream transporters! We bring joy in thirty minutes or less!"

Scattered applause, then more. The twins fanned out and began pelting every table with the glossy, conspiracy-grade flyers. Some of the high-rollers grabbed them and began reading aloud, confusion giving way to hilarity. A pit boss waved a flyer and started chanting, "No bots, more sauce! No bots, more sauce!" The chant caught, echoing through the casino.

Saito, for his part, gave a tiny, cold smile. He reached into his jacket and pressed a button on his lapel.

A chorus of heavy footsteps clanged down the corridor as a fresh wave of security flooded the floor: not just the human guards this time, but a battalion of prototype AI pizza bots—new, shiny, and ominously blank-eyed, each painted in the casino's signature red-and-gold livery.

Lenny's confidence wobbled. He glanced at Tony, who said only, "Time for Plan B."

There was no Plan B.

But then Tony, as if reading from a private script, grabbed the closest pizza—still bubbling, fresh from the casino's oven table—and lobbed it with the grace of a seasoned Little League pitcher. The pie sailed over the heads of security and nailed Slick Vic in the face, dead center. The impact was beautiful: a perfect bullseye of sauce and pepperoni, the pizza splitting in two, Vic's eyes blinking in slow-motion confusion as he fell backwards, cheese slithered down his sharp collar.

For a second, the entire room paused. Then the dam broke.

A second pizza flew from the pizza co-workers; it caught a security guard in the chest and splattered. Scylla took aim with a breadstick, jabbing it so hard into an AI bot's "mouth" that the robot began to whirr and spark. Uncle Red, undeterred by baguette loss, body-checked a guard into a pyramid of parmesan shakers, then used the distraction to liberate a bottle of Chianti from a nearby busboy and quickly splashed it onto another bot, igniting a shower of sparks that lit up the room like fireworks.

"Pizza brawl!" Lenny shouted, channeling his inner gladiator.

Instantly, everything went full tilt.

Pizzas, calzones, garlic knots—anything with aerodynamic properties—became projectiles. The bots, programmed for "maximum efficiency," responded by arming their built-in sauce dispensers and dousing the rebels with pre-heated tomato artillery. But the bots' targeting was off; they mostly hit the millionaires and their own staff. Khadijah, ducking for cover, shrieked as a jet of alfredo took out her entire left sleeve.

"Not my casino," Saito yelled as he took to cover.

Olu, veteran of a thousand casino showdowns, overturned a roulette table and used it as a shield. "My friend, you have to admire the chaos!" he bellowed, then used his protein shaker as an impromptu grenade, beaning a bot square in its LED display. The robot staggered, repeated, "Order confirmed. Order confirmed," and then spun out, knocking over a line of high-rollers like bowling pins.

Kim So-yeon dove under the main table, yanking her tablet and a tangle of cables behind her. She plugged into the nearest bot, fingers flying in an attempt to rewrite its code. Instead, it began shrieking, "PINEAPPLE TOPPING ON ALL PIZZAS. ERROR. ERROR," in a loop, until two of the twins subdued it with a cheese-laden bear hug.

Through it all, Lenny stayed atop his table, ducking pies and projectiles. He'd lost the chef's hat somewhere in the opening salvo, and his beard was already clotted with ricotta and green peppers, but he kept the speech going.

"We are not obsolete!" he bellowed, as a slice of sausage whizzed past his head. "We're the ones who know your kids' names! Who remembers you like extra napkins! We're the hands that carry your midnight cravings to the door!"

Uncle Red, now dual-wielding Chianti bottles, did a slow-motion slide across a slick of garlic butter and knocked the feet out from under a casino manager. Scylla commandeered a pizza cart, rammed it through a line of bots, and cackled as they toppled like dominoes. Nick, after failing to hit any guards with a thrown calzone, just started eating his ammo.

Even the casino's regulars got into it. A retiree at the blackjack table grabbed a pepperoni token and flung it like a ninja star at one of the malfunctioning bots, which began to strobe and yell, "NEW CUSTOMER DETECTED. NEW CUSTOMER DETECTED," until it shorted out in a cloud of oregano smoke.

Within three minutes, the entire casino floor was a war zone: cheese clung to the chandeliers, sauce rivers oozed between the tiles, and the air was a haze of airborne flour and righteous rebellion. It looked, Lenny thought, exactly like the end of the world should.

He clambered higher, standing on a chair atop the pizza table, and raised the briefcase overhead.

"This is for every delivery driver who ever made it on time!" he shouted. "This is for Tony! For Scylla! For the next generation, who might never know the glory of a well-timed knock on the door!"

The crowd—pizza-stained, battered, and grinning—roared in approval.

Olu, pinned under an overturned salad bar, managed a thumbs-up. Kim So-yeon, face streaked with pesto, looked at Lenny and said, with deadpan certainty, "Statistically speaking, this is the best day of your life."

Even Saito, sitting in the wreckage of his own empire, let out a low, grudging laugh.

Lenny looked around. He took it in: the casino, the chaos, his friends, the whole crazy city on the edge of morning.

"We deliver. No matter what," Lenny shouted, as he raised the briefcase one last time.

The sun cracked the window, flooding the room with gold. And for a single, glorious moment, the world made perfect sense.

He jumped down into the crowd and grabbed his own pizza to toss.

Somewhere, in the wreckage, a pizza bot twitched, then spoke its final words.

"Enjoy your pie. Tip your driver. Thank you for choosing human."

Streaming Justice

For a split second, the aftermath of the opening salvo hung in the air: cheese fusing with crystal chandeliers, red sauce arcing in slow motion from ceiling to carpet, bots short-circuiting and spinning out into the arms of retirees and high rollers alike. And then, as if the universe needed a final nudge, Scylla—the pizza co-worker who had, until now, specialized in posting "accidental" food injuries to TikTok—shrieked with glee and held her phone aloft. The little red "LIVE" dot blossomed in the upper corner, and with it, the world was invited to the absolute worst day of Mr. Saito's life.

The casino's side stage, built for tacky cover bands and mediocre magicians, became Scylla's command post. She scaled the steps, phone outstretched, panning across the floor with the steady hand of a seasoned documentarian or possibly just someone who'd streamed a lot of backyard wrestling. Her commentary was a relentless barrage of pizza puns.

"Yo, it's carnage at the Saucy Casino—this is a full-blown pizza coup! That's Lenny Bruno, he's the one in the sauce-camouflage," she narrated, her voice cutting through the riot like a cheese wire through provolone.

The camera caught the twins first, Pink #1 and Pink #2, hair neon as the casino's LED strips and faces set in identical masks of pure, caffeinated glee. They moved as one, raiding the buffet line for ammo and launching slices with the aerodynamic precision of Olympic frisbee champs. Their technique was half sorority food fight, half synchronized SWAT operation, and entirely impossible to counter. Every toss was punctuated by a war cry—"YEETZA!"—and every landing left a trail of sauce and toppings that redefined the room's color palette.

Lenny had fully embraced the chaos, and he figured it was time to unleash payback for all that had occurred to him this night. He crouched behind an upturned mozzarella-stick craps table, clutching the battered briefcase as if it were a fragile kitten. Every few moments, he peeked over the edge, launching whatever he could grab: meatballs flew through the air like cannonballs with unexpected precision, and once, in a moment of pure irony, he hurled a handful of salad greens that scattered like confetti.

A sausage link smacked him squarely on the ear; he stumbled but quickly regained his footing from the odd wet willy. Immediately, retaliating by splattering blue cheese dressing across the nearest security guard with a wild grin on his face and shrugging as if to say, 'It's your fault you came.'

All around, the décor that Saito had spent a small fortune perfecting was transformed into a war zone of culinary mayhem. Pepperoni slices stuck to every available surface, curling and burning under the hot lights like edible shuriken. Cheese dripped from the chandeliers in long, lascivious strands, giving the room an ambience somewhere between "wedding gone wrong" and "Frankenstein's fondue." The gold-trimmed slot machines glistened beneath a coating of parmesan, while the roulette wheel, knocked askew by a flying pizza stone, spun endlessly, a coin perched at the edge of a black slot, refusing to tip.

The millionaires, arrayed at the far end like a particularly well-funded firing squad, finally took action. Saito stood first, rising from his throne of pizza boxes. His eyes, normally flat and unreadable, burned with the cold focus of a man who once beat a Yakuza enforcer in chess while hosting a dinner party. He surveyed the chaos, teeth flashing as he barked a single word: "Enough."

But the room was past listening.

Khadijah al-Hari, never one to be upstaged, launched a riposte by flipping an entire table of artisan flatbreads into the melee. It landed with a crash, sending gluten-free shards flying and shattering a row of commemorative beer mugs. She adjusted her gold nose ring, flicked a stray olive from her braid, and glared at the nearest bot until it powered down in apparent shame.

Olu Goldfinger, not to be outdone, waded into the fray with the confidence of a man who'd once stormed a baccarat pit in nothing but boxer shorts and a smile. He snatched a half-eaten pie from a distracted gambler, flipped it upside down, and used it as an impromptu shield to bull-rush a line of humans. Every few steps, he stopped to deliver a monologue about the dignity of the working class and the sanctity of human error, his Nigerian lilt soaring above the din.

At the edge of it all, Kim So-yeon crouched behind a tower of stacked breadsticks, typing furiously on her tablet with one hand and hacking a pizza bot's firmware with the other. "Statistically, they should have run out of cheese by now," she muttered. When the robot began shooting mozzarella at twice the previous rate, she added, "Correction: I have improved the cheese output."

The camera feed, held high by Scylla, careened between these stations of the cross like a drone with a vendetta. The comments lit up in a rainbow of emojis and screaming hashtags:

#PizzaRevoltSaucyCansino

#DeliverUsFromEvil

#CheeseApocalypse

#LiveFromTheSaucy

The view count climbed by the second, jumping from double digits to hundreds, then thousands, and then into the territory where even Russian bots had to stop and say, "Whoa, that's a lot of content."

Somewhere in the scrum, Lenny made a break for it. He tucked the briefcase under his arm and crab-walked across the floor, dodging ricotta grenades and leaping over toppled chairs. A security bot, newly rebooted and still sticky with chianti, locked onto him and issued a monotone threat: "Halt, unauthorized courier." Lenny replied with a flung breadstick, jamming it into the bot's speaker grill. The machine vibrated, tried to recalculate, then decided to roll with it: "Breadstick detected. Upgrading dietary preferences."

He aimed for the stage, where Scylla was still narrating with the unflagging enthusiasm of a local TV weatherman in the middle of a tornado.

"And here comes the MVP, Lenny B—dodging security, vaulting the roulette, and—ooh!—just took a direct hit from the calzone launcher. That's gotta sting, but he's still up, folks! This is why you don't skip cardio, people!"

The live chat lost its mind.

"SAVAGE" scrolled across in bold block letters. Then:

"He got wrecked and kept going."

"Is that blue cheese in his beard?"

"Tell the twins to do the Yeetza again!!!"

Lenny barely made it to the stage before the next challenger stepped into his path. Slick Vic Castellano, sleeves now rolled, stood blocking the stairs with a lasagna pan held like a riot shield, a smile dawning on his face.

"Lenny, my friend, time for the final audit," Slick Vic said. "Let's see if you balance out."

Lenny, operating on instinct and residual adrenaline, hurled the briefcase up the stairs, then dove for the twin girls' pizza stack. He snatched a wheel of four-cheese deep dish, spun, and used the centrifugal force to launch it at Vic's face.

Vic had just enough time to mutter, "C'mon, not again."

The pan absorbed most of the impact, but the force was still enough to send him stumbling backwards to trip over the step and fall out of sight.

Meanwhile, Lenny continued to scramble past and reached for the briefcase, only to find Pink #2 had already nabbed it and was live-commentating on her own phone.

"This is the best night of my life," she announced, and the internet agreed.

He caught up to Scylla and the twins at the very edge of the stage. For a brief, shining moment, they had the high ground. Lenny, gasping, beard matted with every cheese in the known universe, peered out at the room below. It was a disaster. It was a miracle.

He looked at the phone, saw the comment stream, and realized: the world was watching.

It was now or never.

He squared his shoulders, hoisted the briefcase, and braced himself for whatever came next.

The crowd—if you could call a chaos of millionaires, cops,

robots, casino staff, and a few dozen ordinary Baltimoreans a "crowd"—was locked in that rarest of moments, a full communal pause. Pizza coins pinged off every surface, ricocheting in slow motion as all eyes turned to the stage, to the slot machine throne, to Lenny Bruno, battered and battered but unbowed.

He felt the weight of it—the city, the moment, the briefcase. He felt, for the first time in his life, like he might actually belong at the top of the food chain, even if it was just a very sticky, carb-laden food chain.

Scylla jammed her phone into his hand, activating the selfie cam with a flourish. He caught his reflection: blue cheese streaked across his beard, a sauce-stain forming a Rorschach across his shirt, and the wild, wide eyes of a man who'd finally lost all pretense of giving a damn.

He steadied himself under the hail of pizza coins, held the phone out, and hit the "front-facing camera" option so hard he worried it might crack.

"People of the world," he said, voice hoarse but steady. "This is Lenny Bruno, live from the center of the first-ever Pizza Uprising. If you're just tuning in, here's the short version: the suits wanted to replace us, B-more's finest pizza delivery guys, with bots, with algorithms, with 'delivery optimization' and zero-hour contracts. They said there was no more room for the old ways. For people like me. For anyone who ever got a box of hope at midnight, or saw the face of a guy so desperate for a tip he gave you his own drink coupon."

He opened the briefcase, angling the camera down so that the battered prototype—screen flickering, case warped from the melee—sat center frame. The screen glowed blue, then spat a few sparks, then pulsed with a single, looping video:

A robot, arms laden with pizzas, knocking on a door.

The door never opened.

Behind him, a hush settled over the floor. Even the bots seemed to pause, as if waiting for the punchline.

"They want to make us obsolete," Lenny went on, "but here's the thing: you can't algorithm a soul. You can't code desperation, or hope, or the dumb urge to show up when the odds say you should just go home and order takeout."

He looked around the room, then back into the camera.

"You ever gotten a pizza from a robot? It's cold. It's sad. It never laughs at your dumb jokes or pretends not to notice you wearing pajama pants at four in the afternoon. Robots don't care. They never have to."

The coin storm intensified, tokens pelting the stage and bouncing off Lenny's shoes.

"But humans... humans are a mess. We're unreliable, we're late, we screw up orders, we get lost, we have breakdowns in alleys and cry on the job and sometimes smell like yesterday's anchovies. But we care. We try. We remember your name and your order, and sometimes we risk everything just to bring you a hot slice of something good on a bad night."

The live feed, projected on every screen in the casino, was now joined by a second feed—Scylla's TikTok, then the twins' Instagram, then, impossibly, the local news. Comments scrolled so fast they looked like the afterglow of a shooting star.

"Go off, king!"

"This guy is the people's champion!"

"I'm ordering a pizza RIGHT NOW. Where do I tip?"

Lenny grinned, feeling the briefcase tremble as the prototype inside began to whine.

"Here's my offer," he said. "Invest in your local pizza guy. Your local anything. Because robots can't care, but we can. And we do. And no matter how hard you try, you can't put that in a briefcase."

He held the case high.

"And even if you could—I'd still deliver it."

A wave of laughter rolled through the casino.

"Authorities, if you are capable of anything, please arrest that man," Saito yelled with all his might, seeing the tide had turned. He slumped in his pizza-box throne, lips drawn tight in a line of pure defeat.

With the food fight coming to an end, every police officer in the room converged on the stage.

The prototype, still live, began to spark in earnest. The screen looped the failed delivery video one last time, then went dark. With a sound like a microwave giving up the ghost, the briefcase fizzled, coughed a puff of smoke, and died.

Scylla snatched the phone back, zoomed in on Lenny's face.

"Viva La Pizza," she whispered.

He laughed, raising his hand in a salute, and the world—this messy, hungry, ridiculous world—cheered right along.

The coin storm slowed, the bots powered down, and for a moment, the entire casino froze in time.

Then, as if the universe wanted to give the human race one last, perfect encore, a single slice of pepperoni sailed out of the crowd, arced high above the lights, and landed directly in Lenny's outstretched hand.

He bit in, savoring the moment.

"We deliver," he said. "No matter what."

In an instant, a mass of officers crashes into him, sending him sprawling onto the floor.

From Zero to Hero

If you could bottle shame and pour it over a holding cell, it would look exactly like the intake row at Baltimore's Central Booking, 8:00 a.m., a few hours past sunrise and hours after the world's most embarrassing casino showdown. Lenny Bruno slouched on the coldest, least supportive bench ever engineered by municipal contractors, hands cuffed behind his back, the stink of dried mozzarella and regret slowly rising off his uniform. Next to him, Tony Martinelli sported matching wrist jewelry and a look of righteous martyrdom, as if being arrested alongside his worst employee was the highlight of an otherwise disappointing career.

The twins, Pink #1 and Pink #2, sat with their heads together, quietly debating whether they'd make better memes as criminals or victims. Their chef hats were gone, but the pink dye in their hair had survived the night; it clashed violently with the crusted sauce that had dried to the consistency of terra cotta. Scylla hunched at the end, one shoeless foot tapping an unrepentant rhythm, and flashed a crooked peace sign at anyone who glanced her way.

Uncle Red—still wearing the battered French chef's toque and two layers of fake mustache—occupied the far end of the bench. Despite the cuffs and the obvious swelling on one cheek, he radiated the serenity of a man for whom police custody was neither a novelty nor a tragedy, just a pit stop in the eternal game of street chess.

The room buzzed with the sound of paperwork, printers, and the occasional bleat of a fluorescent light dying a slow, cancerous death. Above the intake desk, a battered TV cycled through news and weather, the volume up just enough to cut through the general misery.

"...in an unprecedented display of civil disobedience—" said the anchorwoman, voice smooth as the glaze on a Krispy Kreme. The screen cuts to aerial footage of Saito's Saucy Casino, now clearly cordoned off, the parking lot still sticky with the aftermath of a night no one would ever fully explain.

The officers on duty had stopped pretending not to stare. One, a beefy patrolman with a handlebar mustache and forearms like turkey legs, took a slow lap of the row and paused in front of Lenny.

"Well, if it isn't the world's dumbest Robin Hood," he said. "You're allergic to following orders, or just to not being a disaster?"

Lenny gave him the tired half-smile he reserved for angry customers and city officials. "I deliver chaos, no extra charge," he said.

The cop snorted and moved on, but not before giving Tony a look of genuine pity. "You used to be a contender, Martinelli."

Tony stared straight ahead. "Still am, just play a different game," he said, as if that was enough to satisfy both cop and conscience.

The news switched to a low-angle, high-definition replay of the casino melee. Slow-motion shots captured every humiliating frame: Pink #2 corkscrewing a pie at a security guard, Scylla somersaulting over a fallen blackjack dealer, Lenny himself on top of the table, wild-eyed, bellowing his manifesto to a crowd that, even in video, looked too stunned to process reality.

"Back to you, Kim," the anchor said, unflappable as ever.

Scylla nudged Lenny with her shoulder. "You looked good, B. Real 'last stand at the Alamo' vibes."

Lenny shrugged, the motion awkward with his hands behind him. "If I'd known they'd use slow-mo, I'd have shaved."

The twins giggled, then launched into an argument about whether his beard made him more or less relatable. Lenny didn't catch the details; he was fixated on the plexiglass evidence bin behind the desk, where his battered phone lay face-up, screen flickering under the relentless siege of notifications.

Even from across the room, he could see it: a steady scroll of pings, likes, and the screaming blue badges of tags gone viral.

Tony followed his gaze. "If you're hoping for a presidential pardon, I think you missed the window, Bruno. The president moved onto the America's Most Wanted list."

Lenny shook his head. "Just trying to figure out if I'm out of a job, or if we all are."

Uncle Red cackled. "Jobs? Kid, after that, you'll never work in this town again. In a good way. You are a legend now. A meme, but a legend nonetheless."

An officer at the booking desk called out, "Next!" and Tony grunted as two guards lifted him to his feet. The intake process was surprisingly efficient, possibly because the staff was desperate to clear the backlog from the casino disaster. Within minutes, all seven members of the Tony's Pizzeria War Council were processed, fingerprinted, and deposited in the next holding area, this one blessed with actual windows and a direct view of the TV.

The morning news had moved on, but not far. Now it was all "Pizza Uprising" and "Cheese-Pocalypse," with every talking head in town weighing in. Some called Lenny a "blue-collar hero." Others labeled the crew "anarchists with pepperoni." The local ACLU rep went on record saying, "It's about time someone stood up to Big Delivery."

Lenny tried to focus on the good press, but the adrenaline had worn off, and what remained was the bone-deep terror that maybe, just maybe, he'd made the biggest mistake of his life.

Next to him, Scylla yawned theatrically. "You think they let us keep the hats? I got, like, two hundred followers begging for mine."

The twins nodded, then harmonized, "If anyone finds ours, DM us, please." They high-fived, perfectly in sync, then settled into a mutual silent sulk.

Uncle Red muttered, "The revolution will be catered," then fell asleep with his mouth open.

The minutes dragged. One by one, the holding area filled with drunks, the unlucky, and a bachelorette party that had apparently crashed a cop bar downtown and refused to leave until someone taught them to tase each other. Their presence improved the general mood, or at least distracted from the stench of feet and despair.

Lenny dozed off, then jerked awake as the news cut to a live feed: a local "man-on-the-street" segment outside the casino, where a parade of witnesses gave wildly conflicting accounts of the food fight. A teenager in a Pikachu onesie raved, "It was beautiful, man, like, real democracy in action." The next interviewee, a businesswoman in an immaculate skirt suit, said, "Frankly, I thought it was performance art. I gave them a standing ovation."

Even the police chief, when asked, "What's your official response?" just shrugged and said, "Frankly, I've seen worse."

Tony watched it all with a kind of cold, academic detachment. Lenny tried to read his face, but the man was a brick oven, heat radiating out and nothing getting in.

A shuffle at the intake door caught Lenny's attention. A man stepped inside—tall, trim, and so out of place in the holding area that he might as well have been an alien. He wore a suit so crisp it could have served as a murder weapon, and the shoes alone were worth more than Lenny's car (back when Lenny still had a car). The man scanned the row, then smiled and approached, cutting through the din like a scalpel.

He stopped in front of Lenny, hands folded behind his back, posture that screamed, "I do yoga, and you don't." His voice, when it came, was velvet over rebar.

"Mr. Bruno?"

Lenny blinked, wary. "Depends who's asking."

The man grinned, a disarming, all-American smile that made Lenny want to punch and trust him in equal measure. "Maxwell Thornton. You don't know me, but I know you. Quite a show last night. Really something special."

Tony leaned forward, squinting. "You a lawyer?"

"Not exactly." Maxwell's smile widened. "Let's just say I invest in talent. And you, my friends, have potential."

Scylla let out a low whistle. "You the bail fairy or something?"

Maxwell turned, giving her a once-over. "If that's what you need me to be, sure. I've already arranged for your release. Charges are... in negotiation."

The holding cell went quiet. Even Uncle Red woke up, sniffing the air for signs of trouble or free breakfast, then spotting Maxwell.

"It's the Feds. Keep your lips zipped," Uncle Red declared, his eyes fixed intently on Maxwell like a hawk zeroing in on its prey.

"Relax, Uncle Red, he's cool," Lenny said.

"If you say so, that's the same thing the aliens thought before being probed."

Lenny rolled his eyes, then turned to Tony, who merely lifted his shoulders in a casual shrug. "Hey, I'd count it as a victory, Bruno."

Before he could process, the officers were back, uncuffing the group and herding them to the exit. They moved in a daze, barely registering the shouts and cheers from the overnight regulars. Lenny's phone was returned, now at 2% battery and vibrating like it was trying to claw its way out of the evidence bag.

Maxwell led the parade to the lobby, then stopped just outside the station doors. The morning was cold and sharp, the kind that wakes you up even when you want to sleep forever.

He turned, hands still folded, and smiled again. "I'd like to buy you all breakfast," he said, as if it were the most natural thing in the world.

Tony glanced at Lenny. "Your call, boss."

Lenny considered. His body screamed for bed, but his brain—always a sucker for a new disaster—said, "Why not?"

Maxwell gestured to a waiting car, doors already open. "Hop in. My treat."

The group piled in, barely fitting. The smell of them—yeast, cheese, defeat—filled the luxury interior in seconds. Maxwell didn't seem to mind. He gave the driver a nod, and they slid away from Central Booking and into the waiting arms of destiny, or at least a very expensive breakfast.

As the car pulled into traffic, Maxwell said, "Let's talk business, Lenny. I think you're just what my portfolio needs."

Lenny snorted, half-amused, half in disbelief. "You want to invest in a washed-up pizza guy?"

Maxwell grinned, wider than ever. "Not just a pizza guy. A man with vision. And a hell of a delivery."

Lenny met his eyes in the mirror. For the first time since the night started, he let himself believe it might all be worth it.

"Then let's eat," he said.

And the car rolled on, carrying the city's most unlikely heroes to their next destination.

Inside a 24-hour diner not too far from Central Booking, Maxwell led the way, head high, suit undiminished by the stench of criminality trailing behind them. He picked a booth near the window, where the squeegeed glass looked out on a landscape of empty parking lots and yawning delivery vans. The group followed in a slow, awkward shuffle, banished to the farthest end of the banquette as if even the vinyl was afraid of what might rub off.

Lenny slid in, feeling the air-conditioned chill cut through what was left of his adrenaline. Tony sat across from him, arms folded tight, jaw working like a piston with every small, defiant clench. Uncle Red, still in full fake-mustache regalia, sprawled at the end, waving at the waitress with the confidence of a man who'd been escorted from better establishments and lived to tell the tale.

The twins took the side seats, instantly pulling out their phones to document the moment. Scylla, ever the iconoclast, perched on the edge of her chair and started peeling the labels off the creamer cups, sticking them on the salt shakers as makeshift armor.

Maxwell, undeterred, scanned the menu with real interest. "Try the eggs Florentine," he suggested. "Actually edible. But the sausage? Unrivaled."

The waitress arrived, eyes darting between the ruined uniforms and the business casual. "You all together?" she asked, tone halfway between disbelief and pity.

Maxwell answered for everyone. "Coffee. All around. And a stack of pancakes—no, two. For the table."

She blinked, then scribbled and hurried away, probably to warn the cook.

The table sat in a chorus of groans and fidgeting. Lenny, already jittery, began sorting the sugar packets by color and lining them up in patterns, as if he could arrange the rest of his life the same way.

Maxwell watched, amused. "You got a system, or is it just for fun?"

"I like to know where things stand," Lenny said with a shrug, refusing to meet his gaze.

Tony grunted. "He means he likes to pretend there's order to the universe, when really, it's just blue, yellow, pink, and suffering."

"Suffering is just a flavor, Tony. Like garlic or debt," Uncle Red chimed in to seize the moment.

The twins snickered, and Scylla raised a plastic creamer as if to toast. "To suffering," she said. "May it always be gluten-free."

The coffee arrived, scalding and unapologetic. Lenny drank it black and fast, burning the roof of his mouth, welcoming the pain as a distraction from the gnawing sense of impending doom.

Maxwell sipped his, then set the cup down with precision.

"I'm going to level with you," he said. "I could sit here all day talking about last night, about the legend of the Saucy Casino, about the way you—" He jabbed a finger at Lenny. "—stole the show and rewrote the rules by going up against some as powerful as Mr. Saito."

Lenny winced. "We're not proud of it. Mostly, we're just glad nobody died."

"On the contrary," Maxwell said, "I've never seen a more effective case for why humans matter. Why real people—imperfect, unpredictable, and very, very messy—are worth more than all the robots, algorithms, and diamond-encrusted billionaires in the world."

Tony rolled his eyes but said nothing.

Lenny felt the gears in his brain stutter, "You do know I'm a walking disaster, right?" then lurch forward.

Maxwell grinned. "That's exactly why I like you. I've spent the last ten years bankrolling 'visionaries' who all want to build the next big thing. They talk about 'disruption' and 'synergy' and 'changing the world,' but not one of them ever changed a tire, let alone a city."

Scylla squirted three sugar packets into her mouth at once, eyes wide. "So what, you want us to start a riot every week?"

Maxwell shook his head. "No. I want you to build something. Something that helps people like you—and me, when I was younger. Something that matters."

Uncle Red tapped a finger on the tabletop, making slow, deliberate circles. "You know what matters? The algorithm. The algorithm is the new Constitution, man. You either code it, or you get coded. You ever seen a pizza delivered by a drone? No soul. No risk. No tip, unless you hack the app."

"We tried to hack the app once. Almost burned down the

phone, but it was worth it for the free breadsticks," Pink #1 chimed in.

"You see? This is what I'm talking about. Grit. Passion. The ability to survive, even when the deck is stacked against you," Maxwell laughed.

"You keep saying 'build something,' but you don't mean a pizzeria, do you?" Tony joined in to finally break his silence.

"Not unless it comes with a social network and a data-privacy guarantee." Maxwell winked. "Look, last night, when Lenny took the stage—when he stood up and said what we all knew but nobody had the guts to say—I realized I was backing the wrong horses. I want to back you."

Lenny could feel the attention gathering around him, even from the waitstaff, who now delivered their food with a combination of reverence and horror. The pancakes landed with a thud, and the sausage links sizzled in their own greasy glory.

He stared down at the food, then at his hands, then at the indifferent world beyond the diner's glass.

"What if I have nothing to offer?" he asked.

Maxwell leaned in. "Then you invent something. You take all that fear, that rage, that absolute refusal to quit, and you do what you do best: deliver."

Uncle Red started to say something, but Lenny cut him off. "Hang on." He grabbed a napkin, flattened it on the table, and began scribbling with a pen from his pocket. The first lines were jagged, desperate; then they smoothed out, coalescing into a grid, then a web, then a logo.

The twins and Scylla peered over his shoulder.

"What is that?" Pink #2 asked.

"It's a gig," Lenny said, words coming faster now. "It's all the gigs. For every person who ever needed a second job, or a third, or a fourth. For everyone who got replaced by an app, a robot, or a manager who didn't know their name. It's a network—no, a highway. Like Uber, but for all the people Uber left behind. It's the," he paused to look up at Maxwell. "You ever heard of Bruno Boost?"

Maxwell's eyes gleamed. "No, but I want to."

"That's because it doesn't exist, at least not now," Lenny kept sketching, manic now. "It's like a platform, but not evil. You sign up, you pick your gigs—pizza, groceries, tutoring, dog-walking, whatever. But it's not the company screwing you over; it's the workers calling the shots. Transparent, fair, no data mining, no black-box algorithms. Just people helping people, and maybe making enough to pay the rent."

Tony considered, then nodded slowly. "You'd need safe-guards. Insurance. A way to weed out the psychos."

Scylla cackled. "That's easy. Just put a quiz on the sign-up page. If you answer 'pineapple on pizza,' you're out."

The twins nodded, faces serious. "And it needs a meme section. For morale."

Uncle Red leaned back, hands behind his head. "Bruno Boost. It's got a ring. Better than 'SkyNet,' anyway."

Lenny felt the idea catch fire in his head. "Maxwell, you want to bankroll that? A worker-owned platform, run by the people who use it?"

"I want to put it on every phone in America," Maxwell beamed.

The table burst into a chorus of cheers, coffee sloshing and silverware clattering. For a moment, even Tony cracked a smile.

The sausage and pancakes were devoured in a feeding frenzy, the group already planning logos and slogans and launch parties. Lenny couldn't stop sketching, couldn't stop the ideas from spilling out faster than he could trap them on the napkin.

By the time the plates were cleared, the napkin was covered in blue ink and hash marks, arrows and numbers, half-formed names, and a crudely drawn rocket ship with the words "Boost or Bust" scrawled beneath it.

Maxwell took the napkin, folded it with reverence, and tucked it into his jacket pocket. "You just drew the future, Lenny. I hope you're ready for it."

Lenny stared out the window at the empty street, then back at the wild, battered crew that had somehow become his family. He felt a flicker of hope—small, bright, and just dangerous enough to be worth chasing.

"I was born ready," he said, surprising even himself.

Uncle Red saluted with a creamer, Scylla shot him a thumbs-up, the twins snapped a selfie, and Tony just grunted in approval.

The city waited outside, ugly and beautiful, hungry for the next delivery.

Lenny grinned, and for once, it didn't feel forced.

"Let's get to work," he said.

And they did.

The Neon Spoon's windows, never quite clean but always earnest, flung the morning sun across every chipped Formica surface and battered chrome edge. The city outside had changed costumes: gone was the hungover blue of dawn, replaced with a wild, cloudless gold that made even the concrete look optimistic. Inside, Lenny sat, a little numb and a lot wired, staring at the half-empty coffee cup that now represented his net worth, his reputation, and maybe his last tie to the world that made sense.

Maxwell was on the phone, already prepping for the next phase. "Yes, it's urgent. Yes, today. No, I'm not kidding."

He rattled off a series of instructions that made Tony's head spin and Scylla's jaw drop. "Draft a simple equity agreement— nothing fancy—and email me at this address." He hung up, then checked his watch. "Forty minutes. We'll have a working contract and a prototype landing page. I'll call in the branding guys before lunch."

Lenny blinked, not quite convinced this was real. "What, you got a pit crew waiting in your trunk or something?"

Maxwell grinned. "They owe me a favor. Besides, the world moves fast. We just have to move faster."

The twins, Pink #1 and Pink #2, scrolled frantically on their phones, updating followers with the news: "Bruno Boost, coming soon. We're taking over, one gig at a time." Scylla snuck a piece of bacon, snapped a selfie, and captioned it, "Still criminal, now also CEO."

The waitress returned with an avalanche of food: stacks of pancakes, eggs swimming in butter, links of sausage that glistened with the promise of future cardiac events. She set everything down with a smile that was a tiny bit awestruck.

"I saw you on the news," she said, sliding a syrup bottle into Lenny's orbit. "My kid thinks you're some kinda hero."

Lenny tried to say something modest, but words failed. He settled for, "Thanks. I hope he tips better than most."

Maxwell reached across the table, napkin in hand, and un- folded it like a sacred scroll. "Let's make it official." He scrawled out the broad strokes—percentages, titles, promises of "good faith and no corporate weaselry." When he finished, he slid it to Lenny, along with a pen that looked suspiciously like it had been borrowed from a bank teller.

"Sign here," Maxwell said, tone half-joking, half deadly serious.

Lenny's hand shook. He looked at Tony, who shrugged, "Could be worse. Could be a pre-nup." He looked at Uncle Red, who grinned, "This is how the Illuminati started."

Lenny scrawled his name, shaky but legible. Then, on a whim, dipped his pinky in the syrup and added a sticky, looping "B" at the end.

Uncle Red took the pen, signed as "witness," and drew a spiral underneath, "for luck." The twins insisted on adding emojis next to their names; Scylla drew a skull and crossbones and wrote "No bots allowed."

Maxwell snapped a photo of the napkin, then texted it to everyone at the table. "Now it's legal," he said. "And in the cloud, so nobody can ever delete it."

Lenny stared at the contract, still warm with syrup and the faint, greasy print of Tony's thumb. For a second, he imagined it on a plaque, hanging in some future office, proof that history was built by the desperate and the underqualified.

Outside, delivery trucks rumbled past, engines coughing to life. On the diner's TV, another clip of the casino brawl played—now with a heroic soundtrack and a pundit panel debating whether Lenny was "the last true folk hero" or "an existential threat to the free market."

He looked at the motley crew around him. Even after an all-nighter, after humiliation, police, and the kind of mess that usually ended with an apology tour, they were still here, still hungry. Maybe for food. Maybe for something better.

"So, what now, boss?" Tony grunted.

Lenny stood, feeling the ache in his knees, the syrup sticking to his fingers, and the old, familiar pulse of hope. He thought about everything that had gone wrong and somehow, by sheer accident, it had brought him to this moment.

"We deliver," he said. "Only this time, we deliver for our-selves."

The others cheered, or pretended to, and the twins snapped one last group photo—unfiltered, unscripted, real.

Outside, the city was wide open. The future, too.

Lenny walked out into the Baltimore morning, napkin contract in his pocket and a wild, impossible dream in his head. The sun's warmth hit him like a dare.

He smiled, ready for the next order.

Maybe, just maybe, this time the delivery was guaranteed.

The Prodigal Delivery Boy Returns

Lenny Bruno adjusted the lapels of his brand-new, Bruno Boost-branded blazer—matte navy, that fit him just right, logo stitched just above the heart in clashing orange—and tried not to think about how he looked like a before photo for a motivational speaker's weight-loss program.

If you listened hard, you could hear the future happening just on the other side of the curtain. The roar of the crowd, the hiss of the sound system, the crisp percussion of a hundred MacBooks snapping shut in unison. There were people out there—real people, not just the type who'd been roped into a "soft launch" with the promise of free pizza and commemorative swag. Hundreds of them, maybe thousands, filling every seat in the main auditorium.

Lenny had peeked through a gap in the drape and nearly lost the contents of his nervous system: rows and rows of gig workers in their natural habitat (polyblend polos, permanent under-eye bags), venture capitalists glinting like sharks in $2,000 jackets, and the spiky, kale-eating press corps, some already live-tweeting the keynote before it had even started.

He recognized exactly two faces in the crowd. Tony sat dead center in the front row, wearing a suit jacket over what Lenny was pretty sure was a pizza-stained "Tony's Original" t-shirt. His arms were crossed so tightly he looked like he might wrestle his own shadow. Three seats over, Uncle Red stood out like a protest sign in a Catholic school, rocking a new blue swade tracksuit and his signature knockoff Ray-Bans, even though they'd specifically told him "business casual" at the registration table. He was waving at the stage as if he could already see Lenny through the glare, and maybe he could.

Lenny checked the time on his phone. 09:48. Twelve minutes until his slot, which meant approximately twelve more minutes to die of embarrassment and twelve more to resurrect himself before the opening joke.

He looked down at his hands. They shook like he'd just delivered to a live firing range. He tried to focus on the note cards he'd written in Sharpie (no printer access after midnight, and anyway, ink ran if you sweat on it, which he did, always). The cards looked like ransom notes, sentences cut with thick black lines, some words underlined three times for luck.

He flipped through: "Story of Bruno Boost," "Value Prop," "Why Not Uber?" (circled, angry), and "Closing: Be Human, Not Algorithm." The last one was so sappy it made his stomach contract, but the branding people had insisted, and so had Maxwell, and besides, it did kind of sum up everything that had happened since the food fight at the Saucy Casino.

The emcee, a startup founder with immaculate hair and the voice of an NPR host ordering oat milk, poked his head into the green room. "You ready, Lenny?"

Lenny flashed the man his best "totally not about to faint" grin. "You bet. Just, uh, reviewing my material."

"Awesome." The emcee gave him a thumbs up and left, already rehearsing the pronunciation of "Bruno" under his breath.

Backstage, the techs were running final checks. Someone adjusted the lights, flooding the wings with surgical blue. A woman with a headset sidled over and clipped a tiny mic to Lenny's shirt, warning him not to "touch it or fiddle, it picks up everything." He nodded, then immediately started sweating on the mic.

He caught a glimpse of the Bruno Boost logo spinning on the massive screen above the stage. It was a dumb logo, if he was honest—a rocketship made of pizza slices, with a smiling face peeking from the cockpit—but it made the crowd laugh and the investors open their wallets, so he'd stopped fighting the design team after the third iteration.

Tony had once told him, "Bruno, if you're gonna be a train wreck, at least do it on schedule." Right now, Lenny was five minutes ahead of schedule and on the verge of derailing spectacularly.

He shuffled his cards again. They slipped from his hands, scattered across the linoleum, and for a moment, he just stood there, watching his career and reputation explode like a deck of fifty-two pickup. He bent down, scrambling to grab the cards before the stage manager noticed. The woman in the headset did notice, but just pressed her lips together and pretended not to.

In the scramble, one card went missing. He scanned the floor. It was the joke—his opener. The one-liner he'd spent all night workshopping with Tony and Red, the line that was supposed to set the tone and show he wasn't just another corporate stooge in a cheap suit. He checked under the table, in the trash, between the folds of his blazer. Nothing. His chest contracted. He tried to remember the line, but his mind was white noise.

"Showtime in sixty," called the emcee, and Lenny felt his

stomach attempt to tunnel out through his shoes.

He took a breath. In, out. He remembered the pep talk Tony had given him.

"You got this, Lenny," Tony had said, voice a perfect blend of threat and encouragement. "Worst case, you bomb and we all go back to making dough for minimum wage. But if you kill it? You're the guy who proved humans are better than algorithms. That's immortality. Or at least a book deal."

Uncle Red, never one to leave a moment unruined, had added, "If you freeze up, just tell them about the goat. Everybody loves the goat story."

He was pretty sure Maxwell would veto that, but honestly, what else did he have?

He squared his shoulders, wiped his palms on his blazer, and stepped to the edge of the curtain.

The emcee's voice boomed out, "Please welcome to the stage the founder and CEO of Bruno Boost, Baltimore's own—"

The rest was drowned by applause. Not polite, not "let's get this over with," but genuine, teeth-rattling, a wave that rolled down the rows and straight up into Lenny's sinuses.

He blinked, blinded by the first shock of stage lights. He could make out a wall of faces, and in the very front, Tony with his arms uncrossed, clapping hard, and Red pumping both fists in the air like he'd just won the lottery.

Lenny stepped out onto the stage, cards clutched in a fist, heart jack-hammering in his chest.

For the first time in his life, he felt taller than the crowd.

And for the first time, they were all there to hear what he had to say.

He cleared his throat. The mic buzzed.

"Hey," he said, and his voice echoed across the auditorium,

loud and clear and, for once, not a punchline. "Thanks for having me. I know you're all busy, so I'll try to deliver in thirty minutes or less."

The crowd laughed, the kind of laugh that said they wanted him to keep going.

And just like that, he was off.

Lenny had always believed in the power of a good story, preferably one with pizza stains and a healthy dose of self-loathing. The trick, he'd learned, was to get the first laugh—then everything else was just riding the wave.

By the time he hit his second punchline ("Honestly, I've been fired from more gig apps than most of you have used, and half of them are now bankrupt, which I consider a win-win"), the audience was with him. He started walking the stage, abandoning his notecards like used napkins and letting the words spill as they came. He could see Tony in the front row, arms now uncrossed, mouth set in what almost looked like pride. Uncle Red had stood up and was holding his phone high, live-streaming the whole thing to the one person who would watch.

"People ask me, 'Lenny, what's different about Bruno Boost? Why would anyone switch from the big guys?' And I tell them, 'Because I remember what it was like to be at the bottom. Like, the actual, literal bottom, scraping change from beneath the car seat so I could buy dinner before my shift.' That's why we built an app where the people doing the work get the first slice. Not the middlemen, not the venture guys, not some algorithm in San Francisco that thinks Baltimore is a typo."

A ripple of applause. The screen behind him flickered to life, showing a graph labeled "Boost Growth Curve." The curve went up, dramatically—more dramatic than Lenny had expected. He paused, almost thrown.

"We started in Baltimore. We figured, if it could make it here, it could make it anywhere. It's been six months, and we have fifty thousand users, two hundred small businesses, and our average wage for gig workers is up thirty-seven percent. Not bad for a bunch of rejects from the world's slowest pizza place."

He heard someone in the audience whoop, and recognized the voice. It was Scylla, out in the cheap seats, waving both hands above her head and flashing a peace sign. On either side of her were the Twins, hair still blindingly pink, both now in matching Bruno Boost t-shirts, their old pizza uniforms long since retired.

Lenny grinned, then pointed them out. "Those are the first four people to ever crash my servers. Give it up for the Tony's Pizza crew."

The spotlight swung to them, and the crowd broke into a wave of applause. Tony nodded, pretending not to care, but his eyes were wet. Scylla dabbed at her eyes with a napkin, and the Twins did a synchronous wave.

"But it's not just pizza," Lenny went on. "It's groceries, pet care, tutoring, odd jobs—if it can be delivered, boosted, or fixed, we've got someone who knows how to hustle. We even have a channel for breaking up with your significant other by proxy, which, fun fact, is more popular in D.C. than here."

The room roared. Lenny glanced at his phone, saw the live stream was trending, and felt the terror in his stomach morph into something close to joy.

He tapped the app icon, and it mirrored on the big screen. "Let me show you how it works," he said. "You log in, pick your gig—maybe it's a ride to the airport, maybe it's fixing a leaky faucet. Maybe it's helping your grandma set up her TV remote because the last guy installed it upside down, and she's been watching Jeopardy! in reverse order for a month. You find your job, you get the rate up front, and you keep the whole thing, minus a flat fee that's lower than the price of a slice. No hidden charges, no tip shaming, no dark patterns."

He flicked through the screens, showing off the features. The interface was simple, the kind of clean that comes from letting workers design the flow instead of UI/UX consultants. He demonstrated the built-in chat ("with actual humans, not bots—unless you want to talk to a bot, in which case, I recommend therapy"), the emergency button for dangerous jobs ("which, in Baltimore, is every job after 10 p.m."), and the leaderboard for "Top Boosters" of the week ("Currently dominated by Scylla and the Twins, but I have faith someone else will dethrone them soon").

He looked up, scanning the crowd. "We wanted to make something that didn't treat people like numbers. So we built the only gig platform that cares if you're having a bad day. If you need time off, or you get sick, or your car dies on a lone dark road, we have a community fund—funded by the profits, not your own paycheck—that helps you get through it. Because, believe it or not, sometimes life happens, and the app should not fire you for it."

A moment of silence, then sustained applause. Lenny saw Tony start to stand, then sit back down as if embarrassed by his own feelings.

Lenny felt the edge of his own emotion, raw and unexpected. He took a breath, then pivoted to the story he'd practiced all week.

"I didn't get here by being the smartest guy in the room," he said. "I didn't even get here by being on time. I got here by failing. Over and over. I got here because when the universe gave me lemons, I tried to sell them as pizza toppings."

That got a laugh, which emboldened him.

"Some of you know the story," he said. "I used to be a pizza guy. Night shift, East Baltimore, rain or shine. Then one day, the world changed. Some billionaires got together, decided they could do it better with bots and drones and apps that knew you better than your own mother. I thought I was finished. I was almost right. But instead of rolling over, I started fighting back."

He let the silence stretch. He thought of the mansion, the card game, the ridiculous briefcase that started everything. He thought of Saito's cold smile and the way the casino had turned into a battlefield of cheese and breadsticks.

"I fought back with the only thing I had—me. My friends. People who wouldn't give up, even when the odds were dumb and the rules were rigged. We made a mess, and we made a point. And in the end, we made this."

He gestured at the screen, where the Bruno Boost rocket circled the city in endless, joyous loops.

"Now, I'm not saying it was easy. There were nights when I wanted to quit. Nights when I thought, maybe the robots were right and I really was obsolete. But then I remembered the best advice I ever got. It was from a self-help podcast I found online. It said, 'If you hit rock bottom, bounce. It's what rocks do.' And if a podcast that came free with a Blockbuster Rewards membership can figure that out, so can we."

The laughter was so loud it shook the risers.

He dropped the hammer.

"Sometimes life throws you a goat—literally, in my case— but that doesn't mean you can't turn it into the mascot for your multi-million dollar company."

On cue, the screen behind him switched to the infamous viral video: the goat that had terrorized him that lone night, now proudly sporting a tiny orange Bruno Boost vest, prancing across a lawn with the confidence of a Fortune 500 CEO. The crowd absolutely lost it. Phones went up, hashtags fired off, and someone in the back started a slow clap that turned into a standing ovation.

Lenny let it wash over him, felt the warmth, the pride, the sense that—just this once—he was delivering something no one could ever take away.

He glanced at his palms, noticing the tremors had finally subsided. With a deliberate motion, he spread his fingers wide, as if letting the words spill out into the universe.

"The difference between failure and success isn't talent, or money, or even luck. It's what you do when you get knocked down. It's whether you give up, or whether you grab the next job, the next chance, the next dumb hope, and run with it. Because at the end of the day, all any of us can do is deliver."

He drew in a breath.

"That's it. That's my pitch. We're not just a company, we're a second chance for everyone who ever flamed out, wiped out, or got left behind. And if you want to join us, or just cheer us on, we'd be lucky to have you."

There was a heartbeat of stillness, a breath where the world went quiet.

And then the confetti cannons erupted. Orange and navy streamers rained down, the logo on the screen pulsing with life, and a hundred phones caught the moment in bursts of digital starlight. The applause was a tidal wave, crashing down from every tier, filling the space with a joy so big it almost knocked

Lenny off his feet.

He staggered back, hands raised in surrender, grinning like a maniac. He could see the crew up front—Tony standing, arms above his head, bellowing like a proud dad at a Little League game; Uncle Red hollering "That's my nephew!" into three phones at once; Scylla and the Twins up on their chairs, screaming as if their team had just won the Super Bowl.

He took it in. Let it fill him, the way a good slice fills every hunger.

He bowed, once, twice, then—on a mad, beautiful impulse— did the "Yeetza!" pose from the old days, double fist-pump and all. The crowd caught on, imitated him, and the gesture became the new sign of victory, rippling out to every corner of the room.

And just as the lights began to fade, just as the emcee took the stage to close out the session, Lenny caught a movement in the very back row. A flash of obsidian suit, a smile that was all sharp edges and diamonds. Saito. Watching, expression unreadable, then gone before the lights came up.

Lenny felt the adrenaline spike, but it wasn't fear. It was the certainty that every game had another round, every success a new challenger. That tomorrow, there'd be another battle, another weird job, another shot at changing the world one delivery at a time.

For now, though, he had the stage. He had his crew. And for the first time in forever, he felt like maybe, just maybe, he'd earned the right to stand in the light.

He smiled, fists raised in triumph.

And the world cheered him home.

We'd Love to Hear From You!

Thank you so much for reading this book—it means the world to us. If you found it helpful, inspiring, enjoyable, or just entertaining, would you take a moment to leave a review? Your feedback not only helps others but also keeps us motivated to create more valuable content for you.

Here's how you can leave a review:

1. Scan the QR code on this page, to go directly to the review page.
2. Or, visit Amazon, find this book, and click "Write Product Review."

Also by Gibbs Publishing Conglomerate

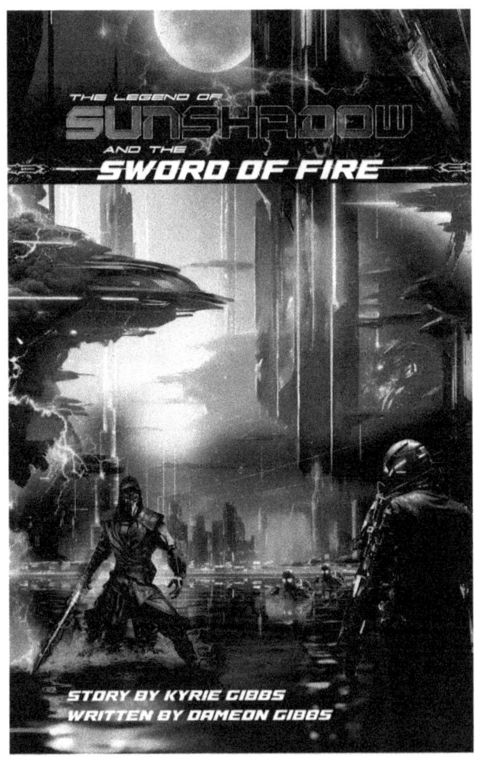

Embarking on a thrilling space adventure, The Legend of Sunshadow and the Sword of Fire, *chronicles the quest of Jubei Hattori, known as Sunshadow, a seventeen-year-old ninja, as he works to retrieve a stolen jewel with the power to control elements. His former temple brother, Nightblade, is responsible for the theft and Sunshadow must use his mystical bracers to summon the legendary Sword of Fire in order to confront him. Along the way, he encounters alien species, forms new alliances, and faces off against the menacing Shadow Lord who threatens the entire universe. As secrets and betrayals come to light, Sunshadow's skills are put to the test as he grapples with the true nature of good and evil and fights to save the cosmos from darkness.*

A large chunk of the world's population was wiped out in the fires of a meteor shower that pummeled the surface. As the world cooled: Ice, famine, and disease took another portion. Now all that roams the planet are the survivors; the ones with the skill, grit, and intelligence to make it another day. On the frozen land, that was once known as England, battles are fought everyday between man and beast. To former mercenary Marcus Rowan, there is no distinction between the two. His team's survival is due to their ability to prepare and handle the worst man, and nature, can throw at them. However, when they arrive in London, Rowan and his team soon discover that they will not only encounter what survived the old world, but also what was born in the new world. Something more dangerous than anything they could have anticipated.

183

The protagonist, Antonio, accepts an under-the-table job flying a helicopter, reminiscent of his military days. The seemingly straightforward task of transporting a package from point A to point B in rural Minnesota becomes a high-stakes adventure, especially when a deadly winter storm sweeps in. The authors create a palpable sense of tension and suspense as Antonio grapples with the decision to risk his life for what initially appeared to be easy money. Will he be able to successfully navigate the helicopter through the blinding, severe snowstorm? How will he survive being on the brink of death?

www.ingramcontent.com/pod-product-compliance
Lightning Source LLC
Chambersburg PA
CBHW041055310726
48978CB00011BA/578